**She was trapped.**

The basement was dank and smelled of mildew.

She'd been foolish to reenter the house, and now Joachim was upstairs with her former captor, giving her her only chance to escape.

Muffled voices came from the kitchen, followed by footfalls as the men exited the house.

Sarah started for the stairs...but stopped when a scratching sound came from the other side of the basement. Though she had little time to waste, she followed the sound to a padlocked door.

She tapped on the door. The scratching came again, and her heart stopped. Knowing she had to be careful, she put her mouth to the door and whispered, "Can you hear me?"



Silence.

She glanced out the window. Joachim couldn't keep her captor occupied much longer. She had to get out now.

She gripped the handrail as a wave of vertigo swept over her. The walls started to cave in around her in a sweep of claustrophobia.

Then she heard it. Her captor's footsteps nearing the basement door. She glanced up just as the doorknob turned.

**Debby Giusti** is an award-winning Christian author who met and married her military husband at Fort Knox, Kentucky. Together they traveled the world, raised three wonderful children and have now settled in Atlanta, Georgia, where Debby spins tales of mystery and suspense that touch the heart and soul. Visit Debby online at debbygiusti.com, blog with her at seekerville.blogspot.com and craftieladiesofromance.blogspot.com, and email her at Debby@DebbyGiusti.com.

**Books by Debby Giusti**

**Love Inspired Suspense**

***Amish Protectors***

*Amish Refuge*
*Undercover Amish*
*Amish Rescue*

***Military Investigations***

*The Officer's Secret*
*The Captain's Mission*
*The Colonel's Daughter*
*The General's Secretary*
*The Soldier's Sister*
*The Agent's Secret Past*
*Stranded*
*Person of Interest*
*Plain Danger*
*Plain Truth*

Visit the Author Profile page at Harlequin.com for more titles.

# Amish Rescue

Debby Giusti

HARLEQUIN® LOVE INSPIRED® SUSPENSE

Recycling programs for this product may not exist in your area.

ISBN-13: 978-1-335-49030-8

Amish Rescue



This edition published by arrangement with Love Inspired Books.



www.Harlequin.com

**Printed in U.S.A.**

Then spake Jesus again unto them, saying,
I am the light of the world: he that followeth me
shall not walk in darkness, but shall have the light of life.
—*John* 8:12

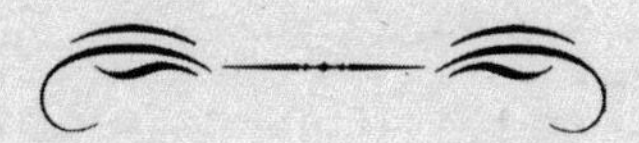

# ONE

Sarah Miller's heart pounded in sync with the footsteps that echoed up the stairway leading to the third story of the old antebellum home. Rats scurried in the attic as she crouched in the closet, pulled her knees to her chest and fought back tears that burned her eyes. The rats didn't frighten her, but Victor Thomin did.

The shuffle of his feet on the landing signaled his approach. Keys rattled as he unlocked the door, sending another wave of panic to ricochet along her spine. The locks—all three of them—were to protect her from those who hoped to do her harm…or so Victor claimed.

"Sarah?"

Her lungs constricted at the sound of his voice. She gasped, struggled for air and wished she could be anywhere except in his mother's house, where he said she was safe.

The door creaked open.

In her mind's eye, she could see his pallid skin, deep-set eyes and shock of red hair as he glanced around the room.

"Where are you, Sarah?" Anger rose in his voice. "Are you hiding from me?"

He knew too much about her, about being left alone as a child, about the fire and the fear that continued to eat at her even though she should know better. Why had she told him so much in her drugged stupor? At least he no longer forced her to take the pills.

"You can't hide from me, Sarah." His voice made her tremble all the more.

The closet door flew open. She startled, gasped for air and wanted to run but was too frightened to move.

He grabbed her arm.

"Don't hurt me." She struggled to pull free. "It was the dream that made me hide."

"Did you dream of being dragged from the car along with Miriam?" he asked, seemingly concerned. His hold eased. "Tell me about it, Sarah."

His voice was syrupy sweet now. How could he be such a Jekyll and Hyde? Hateful one minute, feigning compassion the next.

If only she could remember all the details of the carjacking instead of hazy flashes that clouded her mind.

He leaned closer. "I told you about the bad men, Sarah, the men in your dreams. They captured your sister, but I'm working to get Miriam back before she's transported so far away that you'll never find her again."

Sarah's stomach roiled, sickened by the horrific thought of her sister gone forever. All her life, Sarah had relied on Miriam in times of need. But it wasn't just Miriam she could count on. Even her eldest sister, Hannah, had offered support, though the two of them had not been as close.

"If Miriam can't help me, then Hannah will."

He clicked his tongue. "She left you years ago. Remember, you told me how you cried after Hannah was gone."

Frustrated that he had manipulated even that information from her, she raised her chin in defiance. "I don't believe what you said about Miriam. You're wrong, Victor. She hasn't been taken away. She'll save me."

Sarah eyed the open door to the hallway. Without thinking, she shoved past him and ran toward the stairs.

He chased after her, grabbed her arm and threw her down.

Her shoulder crashed against the floor. She groaned, then scrambled to her feet. He caught her hair and yanked so hard she thought her scalp would rip from her skull.

His other hand wrapped around her neck; all the while he pulled her hair until her face pointed to the ceiling, exposing her throat, where his fingers tightened, constricting her airway.

She clawed at his arm and kicked, her lungs on fire. She couldn't swallow, couldn't scream.

"Don't ever doubt me, Sarah."

Hot tears seared her eyes. She tried to nod, but the movement caused more pain along her scalp.

Her ears rang, something gurgled in her throat, blackness swirled around her. Her knees gave way. In the split second before she would have slipped into unconsciousness, he released his hold. She fell to the floor, gasped for air and clawed her way back to reality.

"Are you going to obey me?" he demanded, standing over her, hands on his hips and eyes glaring.

She opened her mouth, hoping he hadn't seriously damaged her vocal cords. A raspy "Yes" filtered out along with a whimper.

"That's my good Sarah."

She wasn't good and she wasn't his. She never would be. After her mother's transgressions, she would never belong to any man, and especially not a crazed lunatic who had suddenly become abusive. His verbal threats had unnerved her and made her tremble, but until today, he had never touched her inappropriately or raised his hand in anger. Seemingly in the blink of an eye, all that had changed. She couldn't fathom why. The only thing she did know was she needed to escape from Victor's control.

Not that she'd had an opportunity to elude him in the past. He kept close watch on her during the day and made sure she was locked away each night.

With a huff, he yanked her to her feet. "Mother has been asking for you."

"She wants Naomi." From what Sarah could tell, Naomi was a local Amish woman who had taken care of Ms. Hazel before Victor had brought Sarah here. Ms. Hazel repeatedly asked for her.

"You're taking Naomi's place."

Something in his tone chilled Sarah to the core. "Wh-what happened to Naomi?"

His gaze turned somber. "She disappeared, leaving Mother brokenhearted."

More likely, Victor had arranged for Naomi's disappearance.

He touched Sarah's cheek. She turned her head away.

"Listen to me." He grabbed her jaw and forced her to look at him. "A man is bringing your sister here in a day or two. I'll pay George off. Then you and Miriam can take care of Mother together. If you want to see your sister, do as I say."

His thin lips twisted into a hateful smirk. "But if you disobey me, if you try to escape, I'll—"

He let the threat hang.

She uttered the first question that came to mind. "Then will I disappear like Naomi did?"

He bristled.

Evidently, she had struck a chord that rang a little too true.

"I'm not afraid of you, Victor." Could he hear the tremble in her voice?

He leaned closer. "What if I turn off the power and use candles to light the house? Remember what you told me about the fire when you were a little girl?"

Her chest constricted. She struggled to pull air into her lungs.

"Do everything I say, Sarah, so you and Miriam can be together again, and so you can be safe. Do you understand?"

She cocked her head and furrowed her brow as if listening to a rustling sound coming from the unfinished portion of the attic.

He bristled. "What's wrong?"

"Do you hear them?" she asked, feigning an unfounded confidence in her voice.

His face blanched.

"Rats, Victor. They're in the attic."

"I don't believe you."

The fear that flashed from his eyes proved what Sarah had assumed was true.

"Feed Mother her breakfast," he ordered as he hurried out of the room.

From the open doorway, Sarah watched him race down the stairs to save himself from the rats. If she could only escape as easily.

Her momentary euphoria at having unsettled him was short-lived. Exhausted from lack of sleep and weeks of confinement, Sarah dropped her head in her hands. Hot tears burned her eyes. Would she ever be free again?

"Send someone to help me, Lord," she pleaded, her heart breaking at the hopelessness of her plight. "I don't want to die trapped in this old house."

Joachim Burkholder guided the buggy along the mountain road. He had come home like the prodigal son. Except he had not squandered money or lived a life of debauchery. He was, instead, coming home to reconcile with his father. At least that was his plan.

Metanoia, some called it, a conversion or transformation, which was what Joachim had started to experience. Now, he needed to piece his broken life back together. He had tried to live *Englisch.* His heart remained Amish.

Jostling the reins, he encouraged the mare forward. Together he and Belle had traveled from farm to farm to farm. Joachim had worked odd jobs and saved his earnings until his yearning to come home had caused him to slowly retrace his steps.

Belle increased her speed as Joachim took in the rolling hills and lush valleys. How deeply he had missed the beauty of this land and the serenity of the Amish way of life.

Gott, he silently prayed, *forgive my obstinate pride that forced me away from family and faith when I sought to place my will above Thy own.*

The tranquil setting soothed Joachim's troubled soul. He breathed in the loamy scent of Georgia clay mixed with fresh pine from the trees that dotted the side of the roadway. The cool morning air tugged at his black jacket and lulled him into a sense of peaceful calm that dissipated as soon at the buggy rounded the bend. At the bottom of the incline, a level plain stretched out in front of him. His gut tightened as he recognized this particular section of the road home he had inadvertently taken.

Was he trying to add more burden to his already guilt-laden shoulders? Why had he guided Belle to the very spot he had never wanted to pass through again? Some memories were too hard to bear.

He glanced back, debating whether to turn around, retrace his journey and take the longer route that would circumvent this place of pain.

Joachim squared his shoulders, refusing to cower. He needed to face the past to heal. He felt sure that was the advice the bishop would provide when and if he sought to return fully to his Amish faith.

As he turned his gaze to the intersection ahead, Joachim's chest constricted. The morning sunlight filtered through the gray sky overhead, yet for a moment, he stepped back in time as the memory of that night assailed him. He heard the rhythmic clip-clop of horses' hooves against the pavement and the creak of the two buggies as they strained along the ill-fated path.

In his mind's eyes, he saw Eli turn and laugh at Joachim, who followed close behind in the second buggy. The ongoing competition between the two brothers had taken a tragic turn that night.

At eighteen, Joachim should have known better than to go along with the seemingly innocent challenge. He did not blame his brother. Nor had his *datt* blamed Eli. Instead, his father had blamed Joachim.

Once again, he remembered how Eli had egged him on, ignoring the roar of the oncoming vehicle and the headlights speeding too fast.

Joachim had raised his voice in warning. "A car approaches on the road." But Eli had not heard and had not reacted.

The crash of metal and splintering wood echoed in Joachim's memory, along with the horrific cry that had come from his own throat as he screamed his brother's name.

Five years had passed, yet Joachim's grief was still so raw. "*Gott*, forgive me," he whispered as he hurried Belle through the intersection.

Perhaps coming home to the mountains had been a mistake. What had happened could not be undone. No matter how Joachim tried to reconcile the past.

He needed longer to decide if he was ready to contact his father. Work would help. Using his hands and carpentry skills to transform disrepair into integrity would allow him to see more clearly. If he could hole up somewhere, he might be able to stem the figurative bleeding of his wounded heart and come to terms with his future and the way he wanted to live his life.

Belle flicked her head.

"You want to go home, girl. I know. But I need more time."

The turnoff to the old Thomin homestead appeared in the distance. The house had needed work five years ago. If Hazel Thomin were still alive, the elderly lady might hire Joachim to do odd jobs around the property while he tried to decide how he was going to piece his life together.

He pulled back on the reins to slow Belle's pace, then nudged the mare onto the path that led to the grand home. The property had been in Mrs. Thomin's family for generations, but what he saw made his spirits plummet even more. The house that had been regal in its day—some called it a mansion—now appeared wasted from neglect.

Joachim grimaced, noting the peeling paint and the sagging facade. The stately beauty had come under hard times and was in need of a steady hand that could restore her original beauty as well as her once-sturdy understructure.

He guided the buggy toward the front of the house and glanced up to see a young woman near Joachim's age peering from a second-story window. Blond hair hung around her slender face. She stared at him, wide-eyed, for a long moment. His chest tightened in response to the need he recognized, even at this distance, in her pensive gaze.

Before he could acknowledge her presence, she stepped away, leaving him confused by the tangle of emotion that wrapped around his heart.

Joachim pulled the horse to a stop and jumped to the ground as the front door opened. Victor Thomin stepped outside, coffee mug in hand. Tall and skinny with unkempt red hair, Hazel Thomin's only child had not improved in looks—or, it seemed, in temperament—over the last five years.

With a surly grunt, Victor raised the mug to his lips and drank deeply, his beady eyes intent on Joachim, even as he wiped the back of his hand over his thin lips. A cut festered that had spattered his knuckles with dried blood.

Recalling the baleful glance of the woman at the window, Joachim made a connection that caused his eyes to widen in horror—though he immediately reminded himself that it could be wild speculation and not credible in the least. He had no proof of abuse, yet Joachim could not and would not ignore his instincts. Victor had been a scoundrel in his youth, and from the downward pull on his drawn lips, there was no reason to think he had changed.

Extending his hand, Joachim introduced himself. Instinctively, he knew from Victor's menacing expression that the red-haired man had failed to recognize him.

Victor reluctantly accepted the handshake. "Is there something you want?"

"I'm looking for work." Joachim glanced again at the overhead window, feeling a sense of loss at finding it empty. "Carpentry, painting or any handyman jobs you might need done. I can provide references."

Victor pursed his lips. "You're from around here?"

Joachim would not lie, but he saw no reason to provide more than a minimum of information. "I worked in North

Carolina for a number of years. Folks said there might be jobs in this area of North Georgia."

He studied the once-beautiful home, pausing to gaze at each window, hoping for another sign of the illusive woman. "Looks like they were right. Your house could use a bit of upkeep."

Victor shrugged. "I doubt this old place is worth the effort."

"A few repairs will make a big difference," Joachim assured him. He touched the dry rot around the front door and peered inside the house through the sidelight. His heart skittered in his chest.

The woman he had seen moments earlier now stood poised on the landing. She raised her index finger to her lips as if pleading for him to remain silent about her whereabouts. The furtive look on her oval face made him even more concerned about her wellbeing.

Joachim turned back to Victor. "I can do as little or as much as you want. But you should know that the value of your property would improve with the repairs, in case you decide to sell any time soon."

Victor arched a brow. Seemingly, the mention of financial gain brought interest. "You think I could find a buyer?"

Joachim nodded. "*Yah*, if you are willing to fix some of the problems."

"I've got rot around the back porch, too," Victor volunteered. "Plus, the kitchen door is warped and won't close easily."

"Let me have a look," Joachim suggested. He motioned Victor to take the lead and then glanced again into the house. The woman had disappeared.

Joachim sighed at his own foolishness. He knew better than to play hide-and-seek with an *Englisch* woman. He needed employment, not involvement in a domestic dispute. Although she and Victor seemed an unlikely match. Perhaps she was a caregiver for his mother. Still, something did not seem right. Whether she was there as an employee, a spouse or a guest…no woman should look so afraid.

After rounding the house, Joachim climbed to the back porch. Quickly he inspected the sagging roof and rotting soffits, trying to get his mind off the woman who continued to tug at his heart.

His gaze turned to the kitchen window. He stepped closer in pretense of examining the sill, all the while peering through the glass, searching the kitchen and hallway beyond for some sign of the woman.

Victor stood to the side. "If I do hire you," he warned, scratching his chin, "I won't stand for laziness or slipshod work."

Movement caught Joachim's eye. Something or someone hurried across the entrance hallway to the front door.

"I understand your concern, but you will not find me to be lazy or my work slipshod," Joachim said, hoping to keep Victor's attention on the disrepair instead of what was happening inside the house.

Feeling the need to provide a distraction, Joachim tapped the sill and pushed on the wood before moving to the next window and repeating his assessment.

*"Yah,"* he finally said. "There is much work to be done. I could start tomorrow. Pay me only if you are satisfied with the completed job."

"I'll think it over." Victor took another slug of his coffee. "Stop by tomorrow, and I'll let you know."

Joachim nodded. "Sounds *gut*."

Leaving Victor on the porch, Joachim returned to the front of the house. He glanced at the outbuildings and barn in the distance. Had the woman left the house? Was she now hiding close at hand, or was he making more out of that which was innocent?

"Sarah?" Victor's voice sounded as he entered the house.

Joachim climbed into the buggy and flicked the reins. Thankfully, Belle responded with a brisk trot.

Although Joachim kept his eyes on the road, he knew he was not alone. He had seen the tarp—which had been neatly folded and stowed away earlier—strewed over the back of the buggy. Someone was hiding under the thick covering.

He hurried the mare along the driveway and felt a sense of relief as he guided Belle onto the main road.

A sports car raced by, going much too fast. The woman in the passenger's seat turned to stare at Joachim as if she had never seen an Amish man.

Too soon, the sound of another vehicle filled the air.

Joachim looked back, seeing a red pickup truck turn out of the Thomin driveway. Victor sat behind the wheel. The tires squealed as he gunned the engine.

Would he pass by as the other car had done or stop and demand to know who or what was hiding under the tarp in Joachim's buggy?

Coming home had been a mistake. More than reconciling with his father, Joachim needed to reconcile with himself as to why he was so eager to help an *Englisch* woman on the run.

# TWO

Sarah blinked back tears and tried to calm her heart before it ricocheted out of her chest. She had been a fool to think she could escape. The squeal of tires and the whine of a vehicle approaching the buggy made her realize the full extent of her mistake.

She curled into an even smaller ball and prayed the tarp would keep her hidden. After two months of captivity, she shuddered at the thought of what her punishment might be if Victor found her. Plus, she had put the Amish man in danger, and now he would be subject to Victor's wrath, as well. The man driving the buggy was innocent of any wrongdoing and had stepped, quite literally, into a perfect storm that was getting worse by the moment.

That she had grabbed the opportunity to run away from Victor still stunned her. An action she never would have taken if not for his abuse earlier this morning. She had planned to escape with Miriam after they were reunited. Her sister would have known what to do and where to go. Miriam had saved Sarah from the fire. She would have saved her from Victor, as well.

Instead, the Amish man with the broad shoulders and understanding gaze had been the catalyst that had Sarah running for her life. Even when peering down at him from the window, she had felt an instant surge of hope when es met, as if he knew she was in danger and had to her rescue.

he hope evaporated with the deafening roar of the otor vehicle. She fisted her hands and bit down on her lip, willing herself to remain still while internally she wanted to kick her feet and wail like a small child who didn't want to be punished for some misdeed. Yet she had done nothing wrong.

Victor was the one at fault, a fact she needed to remember. How thoroughly he had filled her mind with lies so that she sometimes confused her innocence with guilt.

"You're the reason, Sarah, that we have to hide from the police," Victor had complained on more than one occasion. "If I didn't need to protect you, I would be free to come and go. Instead, we must hole up and hide out so the corrupt cops won't find you and sell you into slavery along with your sister."

He had brainwashed her with his constant badgering about her guilt. Fear, fatigue and her dulled senses, caused by the drugs he forced on her, had added to her confusion.

Thankfully, today, she was able to think rationally enough to seize the opportunity to escape. Pulling in a fortifying breath, she smelled the musty scent of the tarp mixed with the damp cool air of the encroaching storm. If dark clouds hung overhead, hopefully, they weren't a harbinger of what would happen to her in the next few moments.

Instead of the weather, she focused on the clip-clop of the horse's hooves on the pavement and tried to ignore the blast of a horn and the revved acceleration of the vehicle that forced the buggy to the side of the road.

"Hold up there, Belle." The deep voice of the Amish man quieting his horse should have calmed her unease, but knowing Victor was the reason brought another volley of fear to wrap around her spine and underscored the seriousness of her situation as the buggy came to a stop.

*God help me*, she silently prayed. *Help the Amish man. Save both of us from Victor.*

"Hey, Amish." Victor's voice. "Did you see a woman leave my house?"

"Your *mudder*?"

"Not my mother." Victor's sharp retort reminded Sarah of the caustic tone he often used with her. "A twenty-one-year-old woman wearing jeans and a sweater."

"She is your *schweschder*?" The Amish voice was deep and calming.

"What?" Victor didn't understand.

"Your *schweschder*," the Amish man repeated. "Is your sister the woman for whom you are searching?"

"I don't have a sister," Victor spat. "I'm looking for the woman who works for us, helping my mother. Did you see anyone?"

"A car passed by, heading toward Petersville. A woman sat in the passenger seat. The man driving had a bald head."

"What color was the woman's hair?"

"Blond. This is perhaps the woman you are seeking?"

Victor grumbled. A car door slammed and tires squealed as he drove away. Sarah held her breath and listened to the sound of the engine disappearing into the distance.

"He's gone." The Amish man's voice was low and reassuring. "You can come out now."

He had known she was under the tarp?

She raised the edge of the covering and stared up at a square jaw, furrowed brow and deep-set eyes filled with question.

"Did he hurt you?" he asked.

She hadn't expected his concern or the tears that filled her eyes. "Not until today."

"He will return soon. Plus, a storm is approaching."

She looked at the darkening sky.

"I will take you someplace safe. Do you have family in the area?"

She glanced at a nearby road sign—Petersville 5 miles, Willkommen 30 miles—and shook her head. "My sister will be here tomorrow or the day after. She'll make sure I'm safe once she arrives."

"But today you need lodging," he said, calmly stating the obvious. "Stay under the tarp in case Victor returns."

Without further discussion, he turned his gaze to the road and clicked his tongue. The buggy jerked as the horse responded. Sarah found the sound of the horse's hooves on the pavement and the sway of the carriage mildly soothing.

She didn't know anything about the Amish man, yet he had helped her escape. She had to trust him, at least for the moment. From what she knew about the Amish, they kept to themselves and had little to do with law enforcement. If so, the man in the buggy might help her elude the crooked cops who had hijacked Miriam's car and were searching for both sisters even now. He might also help her reconnect with Miriam and take both of them to safety. But where would that be?

Sarah had moved from town to town her entire life with no place to call home except the short-term rentals where she and her mother and sisters had lived for a month or two at most, before moving on to the next temporary lodging. How foolish she was to think her life in the future would be different, no matter how much she longed for stability and a home of her own.

Relieved though Sarah was to be free of Victor, she worried about his mother now left home alone with her crazed son. Over the last few weeks, Ms. Hazel's condition had deteriorated much too quickly, making Sarah wonder if Victor was doing something to speed up her decline.

Concern for the older woman weighed heavily on Sarah's shoulders, but she couldn't do anything to help Ms. Hazel at the moment. Right now, she needed to close her eyes and rest. Sarah had escaped, although she felt anything but free while hiding under the tarp with Victor prowling the area in search of her.

Should Victor return to question her rescuer again, would the Amish man whose faith embraced peaceful nonresistance be able to save her? Or would Victor find her? She shuddered at the thought, knowing that if he got his hands on her once more, Victor would ensure Sarah never escaped again.

The dark sky mirrored Joachim's inner struggle. Passing through the intersection where Eli died had been Joachim's undoing earlier. Now he was hiding a woman he did not know. The added complication only made him more conflicted.

All too clearly, he had recognized the pain on the woman's face as she glanced down at him from the window and again as she stood on the stairway inside the Thomin house, her finger to her lips and her eyes pleading for mercy. Her expression had reminded Joachim of his own sense of hopelessness and despair that had overwhelmed him following his brother's death.

Was that what had drawn Joachim to the woman and made him long to protect her?

He glanced at the rear of the buggy, where she lay under the tarp. By the steady rise and fall of the heavy covering, he presumed she had fallen asleep, which was probably for the best. Fatigue had lined her face along with fear that made him grateful he had come to her rescue.

The wind picked up, and the temperature dropped as dark clouds billowed overhead. Joachim needed to find shelter before the storm brought more chaos to this already confusing day.

He flicked the reins, hurrying Belle. Instinctively, she knew the route he had chosen to take.

The woman needed a place to hole up for a day or two until she could connect with her sister. Petersville was the nearest town, but that was the direction Victor had gone. When he failed to find her there, he would more than likely retrace his route to search more thoroughly in the local area.

The Burkholder farm adjoined the Thomin property, but the road connecting the two homes took a circuitous route around the fields and pastures. Glancing at the sky, Joachim wondered if Belle would get them to shelter in time.

If his father was tilling the soil in the distant acreage, Joachim might be able to signal his sister, Rebecca, especially if she was working in the garden. She had written him faithfully while he was away, telling him about the family. In spite of the breezy news she shared, Joachim had read between the lines, all too aware of the emotional anguish Eli's death had caused his family.

More than anything, Joachim longed to see *Mamm* again, yet his mother would abide by the rules his father established. Having to watch her turn her back on him would be almost too hard to bear.

And the woman hiding in the back of his buggy? If his father forbid Joachim entry into the house, he would hole up in the barn and give the woman as long as she needed to decide where she wanted to go. Until that time, Joachim would stand guard, ensuring Victor did not find her.

But would she want Joachim's help?

He shook his head. An *Englisch* woman was not in his future, yet whether he liked it or not, she was very much in his present. More than anything, Joachim wanted to keep her safe from Victor and from anyone else who might cause her harm.

# THREE

In her dream, Sarah watched Victor raise his hand to strike her. She screamed, then flailed her arms and tried to free herself from the shroud that covered her.

"You are safe." Hands reached for her, removed the heavy covering and pulled her into an embrace.

Not Victor, but the Amish man.

"Shh," he soothed, cradling her like a child.

It was the first comfort she had felt in far too long. She buried her head against his neck, wanting to remain forever enveloped in his warm and protective hold.

Tears filled her eyes and spilled down her cheeks, wetting his cotton shirt. Hearing the rain, she was more than grateful to be under cover and out of the storm, and even more grateful for the human contact.

The rapid thump of his heart proved the Amish man wasn't a figment of her imagination. She nestled closer, not wanting to open her eyes or leave the security of his embrace for which she had hungered too long.

Thunder crashed overhead.

"Joachim?" A woman's voice said the name, her tone filled with surprise.

Another clap of thunder.

Her Amish protector tensed and pulled back ever so slightly.

Sarah clung to him for a moment before her eyes fluttered open.

His head was turned. She followed his gaze to the woman dressed in a calf-length blue dress, white apron and bonnet, who stood just inside the open barn door.

Outside, rain pummeled the earth. The day had turned dark as night. Or was it night already? She wasn't sure how much time had passed. The woman's questioning frown seemed equally dark. Perhaps she was the man's wife. The thought cut through Sarah's heart. She had been such a fool.

Embarrassed by her neediness and the way she had reached out to the man, she untangled her arms from where they had wrapped around him.

He glanced down at her, a glint of confusion flashing from his dark eyes.

Was he upset that his wife had found him giving comfort to a woman who wanted nothing more than to return to his embrace?

"I—I'm sorry," she stammered, trying to make sense of what had happened. "I was asleep. I didn't realize..."

"Who are you?" the Amish woman demanded, glancing first at Sarah and then turning her frosty gaze to the man. "Joachim, is there something you did not tell me in your letters?"

"She needs help, Rebecca."

"*Yah*, and it looks like you need help as well from the way you clutched the *Englischer* to your heart."

"Father is in the house?" he asked, seemingly sidetracking the issue at hand.

Rebecca shook her head. "He and *Mamm* are visiting Aunt Mildred and Uncle Frank in Kentucky. They will be gone for a few more days. Had you written that you were coming home, they might not have left."

Sarah was trying to follow the conversation and understand the undercurrent of what was really being said. The man had mentioned his father. No, his tone implied that it was *their* father. Was the woman not his wife?

"Excuse me," Sarah said, pulling away from him and peering at both of them. "You're not married?"

The woman huffed. "Why do you think this?"

Evidently, Sarah had jumped to the wrong conclusion. She held up her hand. "I'm sorry. I don't want to offend either of you."

She turned to Joachim. "Thank you for bringing me here. If I could stay in the barn until the storm passes, I would appreciate it."

His brow furrowed. "You plan to leave?" He shook his head. "This cannot be."

He climbed from the buggy and motioned to the Amish woman. "We must take our guest into the house."

Glancing back, his gaze burrowed into hers. "Your name is Sarah?"

She nodded. "Sarah Miller."

"I'm Joachim Burkholder." He pointed to the other woman. "My sister, Rebecca."

The weight on Sarah's shoulders lifted ever so slightly. Sister. Not wife. Tears again stung her eyes.

"She needs food and lodging, Rebecca."

The Amish woman stepped closer. Her earlier scowl softened but she seemed hesitant to offer Sarah a hearty welcome.

"We must hurry," Joachim said. "Before Victor returns."

Rebecca grasped her brother's arm. "Victor Thomin?"

"*Yah*. He is staying at his mother's house."

*"Ach,"* his sister groaned, with a shake of her head. "Naomi said he is not a good man."

"You know Naomi?" Sarah asked. "Victor's mother kept asking for her."

Rebecca nodded. "Naomi lived nearby. She cared for Ms. Hazel while Victor was away."

Joachim pointed to the open barn door. "The rain eases. We must go inside."

He reached for Sarah and helped her from the buggy. Taking her hand, he hurried her out of the barn.

Dark clouds rolled overhead. Another storm was approaching, but Sarah breathed in the cleansing air, feeling a sense of relief. She had escaped Victor. She had a place to stay. At least for now, she was free.

A bolt of lightning pierced the sky and struck nearby. The almost-immediate crash made Sarah realize everything could change in an instant.

She would never be free of Victor, not until the hateful man was stopped.

The rain intensified just before Joachim and Sarah reached the porch. Another sound was discernable over the rain. He glanced at the drive and tensed. A horse and buggy scurried along the main road. For a long moment, Joachim stared after the buggy and then let out a deep breath.

"You thought it was Victor, didn't you?" she pressed.

He squeezed Sarah's hand, hoping to provide reassurance and bring comfort to her seemingly still-anxious heart. "Victor will not find you here."

At least that was Joachim's hope.

Together they climbed the steps to the porch. He opened the door and motioned her inside. She wiped her feet on the latched rug and hurried into the kitchen.

A sense of calm and right order enveloped Joachim as he stepped over the threshold and stopped to take in the peacefulness that pervaded the space. Glancing at the familiar furnishings—the table and chairs, dry sink and cabinets—his *datt* had made, Joachim soaked in the aura of home and family he had missed for the last five years.

"Rebecca can brew coffee," he said, hoping his voice did not reveal the mix of emotions that had welled up within him upon entering the house. He turned to the newcomer. "Perhaps you would prefer tea?"

Sarah glanced at Rebecca, who hurried in behind them.

"I have cold cuts and cheese and fresh baked bread if you are hungry."

"Thank you both," Sarah said. "But first, I need to wash my hands and face, if you don't mind."

"Of course." Rebecca pointed to the stairs. "I will take you to the room where you will stay the night. Joachim must tend his mare. We will eat after he returns from the barn."

His sister turned as if to shoo him outside. But despite her prompting, he was slow to head to the door. He did not want to leave the home to which he had only now returned. He also did not want to leave Sarah.

He gently touched her shoulder. "So much has happened, but you are not to worry. Victor is in town, searching for you there."

"And if he comes here?" she asked.

"I will not let him into the house."

Belle needed to be groomed and fed. Rebecca would take care of Sarah until he returned. Still, leaving the house this time was almost as hard as leaving the mountains had been five years ago.

How could he have grown so attached to a woman—an *Englisch* woman—in such a short period of time? He knew nothing about her except that she needed a safe place to stay for a day or two. He and Rebecca would open their home to her, but Joachim needed to be careful. As taken as he was by her in such a short time, he feared what might happen in the days ahead. He must guard not only Sarah, but also his heart.

# FOUR

Joachim had said that he would keep her safe. As much as Sarah wanted to believe him, she was worried. Victor was unpredictable, and his mood swings had grown progressively more extreme. He had warned her never to leave him, but she'd done just that. Given how angry he'd been before over smaller infractions, what would his response be to this?

Rebecca filled a pitcher with water and motioned for Sarah to follow her. "A diesel pump runs our well, so we always have water in the house," the Amish woman explained as they climbed the stairs. "Propane heats our water for washing and bathing. Later I will fill a tub for you."

On the second floor, she ushered Sarah into a small but spotlessly clean bedroom. A beige patchwork quilt pieced with blue triangles covered the single bed. A chest of drawers, table and straight-back chair filled the room.

Rebecca placed the pitcher on the chest next to a large porcelain bowl. She opened the bottom drawer and pulled out a thick terry-cloth towel, a bar of soap and a glass bottle.

"I made the soap and shampoo and added natural oils to both products. I hope you will find them to your liking."

"Thank you, Rebecca. You and your brother have been so thoughtful."

Rebecca seemed to appreciate the compliment that hopefully would wash away her earlier concern about Sarah. The Amish woman offered a weak smile. Her cheeks glowed pink with a mix of embarrassment and appreciation. "Come downstairs when you are ready to eat."

Sarah glanced at the inviting bed, wishing she could hide under the covers and curl into a ball. Maybe then she wouldn't worry about Victor finding her again. Was she safe here? Sarah needed to learn more about Joachim Burkholder and his Amish family. Thanks to them, she had a place to stay, at least for now.

She scrubbed her face and hands and dabbed water through her hair, appreciating the clean, fresh scent of the bar soap and eyeing the liquid shampoo. Using the bath products Rebecca had made would be a welcome treat, although so much could happen in the hours ahead. Sarah needed to focus on figuring out what she needed to do to remain free from Victor instead of on creature comforts like having a long soak in a hot tub.

After patting her face and hands dry, she returned to the kitchen.

"The coffee is hot," Rebecca said in greeting. "Or as Joachim mentioned, I could make tea."

"He's still in the barn?" Sarah asked, knowing nothing about farm life and feeling somewhat awkward around his sister.

"*Yah*. Joachim feeds his horse before he feeds himself."

"You seemed surprised to see him."

The Amish woman nodded. "He has been gone from our home for a number of years. It is *gut* to have him back again."

"Do you have other siblings?"

"A brother, Eli, died a few years ago."

"I'm sorry."

"It was *Gott*'s will."

Sarah didn't want to think about a loving God taking anyone's life. At the moment, she longed for something to keep her mind on anything other than death. "May I help you prepare the lunch?"

"You can slice the bread. It is cooling on the counter." Rebecca pointed to the raised loaf. A knife lay next to a cutting board.

"It's homemade?" Sarah asked, admiring the plumpness of the loaf and the golden brown crust.

*"Yah."* Rebecca arranged the meat and cheese on a platter. "I always make extra bread and sell it to tourists who stop at our driveway."

Sarah looked out the window, suspicion growing within her. "Do people often come to your house?"

"It is not something that should worry you," Rebecca assured her.

In spite of Rebecca's comment, Sarah couldn't shake off her concern about strangers visiting the Burkholder farm while she stayed there. She continued to peer from the window, hoping for some sign of Joachim—and for no sign of anyone else. The door to the barn hung open, and the interior looked dark and foreboding.

Rebecca claimed Joachim was caring for his horse, but what if she was wrong? Victor could have returned and overpowered Joachim when he wasn't looking. Perhaps Victor was ready to barge into the house and capture Sarah again.

Minutes ticked by, only increasing her worry. "Why is Joachim taking so long?" she finally asked, unable to calm her unease.

"You could go to the barn and ask him yourself," Rebecca suggested. “Or you could join me in the main room where I have my mending. Joachim will come inside shortly.”

Joachim had assured Sarah earlier that she was safe, but it felt to her as if too much time had elapsed since he had left the house. Rebecca moved into the main room and started humming. The tune, a childhood favorite, should have calmed Sarah’s unease. Instead, it only added to her concern. What was she doing in a strange house with people she didn’t know?

She glanced at the oil lamps on the wall, the candles on the sideboard and the matches on the table. Her chest constricted and her pulse raced. A ringing sounded in her ears that failed to overpower the voice screaming through her mind.

*Fire!*

She wrung her hands. The memory of that night so long ago returned, constricting her lungs and leaving her gasping for air, overcome by the same panic that filled her every time she even thought about flames.

She had to leave. Now.

Ever so quietly, she opened the kitchen door and gulped in the damp air, all the while the voice continued to warn her.

While in the buggy, she had seen a sign for Willkommen. Victor had mentioned Miriam was being held somewhere in that area. Their aunt lived in Willkommen, as well. At least that’s what their mother had told them. If Sarah could get to Willkommen, she might find her aunt, and together they could search for Miriam.

She pulled in a fortifying breath and then raced down the steps and scurried past the barn, heading toward the pasture and a line of trees on the far side of the field. She would hide there until the roadway looked clear. Then she would cross to the opposite side where a thick patch of trees flanked the road. Hidden by dense underbrush, she would make her way to the narrow two-lane that veered off from the main road, where she had spotted the sign for Willkommen.

As much as Sarah had appreciated Joachim's help, she couldn't rely on him to keep her safe. He was Victor's neighbor.

She checked the road for cars, saw that it was clear and crossed the pavement. The approach of a vehicle sounded in the distance. Her pulse raced. She turned to glance over her shoulder.

Her heart stopped as a red pickup crested the nearby hill. Victor!

She ran toward the trees, needing to disappear in the brush. She wouldn't let him capture her again.

The truck accelerated.

She ran faster.

The screech of brakes made her heart lurch.

Victor had seen her.

Footfalls pounded the pavement. He was coming after her.

She'd been so foolish. Victor was more of a threat to her safety than the matches and candles and oil lamps. She never should have traded the security of Joachim's house for the outdoors, where she was so vulnerable.

"Sarah!" Victor screamed her name.

She hesitated for a fraction of a second, then chastised herself for being so easily swayed.

Fighting against the pull of his voice, she forced herself forward, remembering how he had choked her this morning until she couldn't breathe.

She pushed through the bushes, needing to escape his voice, his control. To escape him.

"You won't get away, Sarah," he called, as if reading her mind. "I'll follow you. You can't escape from me."

The branches scraped her arms and pulled at her sweater, but she kept going, ignoring the cuts to her flesh. She couldn't listen to her body. She had to listen to her mind, warning her to run fast, run hard, run away.

She made a sharp turn to the right and ran all the faster. The only sound she heard was her own raspy breath and pounding heart. For an instant, she thought she had eluded him until the sound of his footfalls returned along with the rustle of leaves.

If only she had stayed at Joachim's house. He would have protected her.

"Sarah!" He was close. Too close.

She tripped.

He grabbed her.

She fought to free herself from his hold.

*No!* She tried to scream, but his hand clamped around her mouth.

"Sarah?" Victor called again. This time, he was farther away and moving in an opposite direction.

If Victor wasn't holding her, then who was?

Soft. Her skin was so very soft.

Joachim dropped his hand, releasing Sarah from his hold.

She stood ever so still, as if afraid to move.

"He's heading back to his truck," Joachim whispered. "You lost him when you made that sharp turn to the right. I saw you cross the street when I left the barn, but it took me a while to catch up to you."

"Oh, Joachim," she said, pulling in a deep breath. "Victor was following close behind me."

"But you outsmarted him, Sarah."

She turned to gaze up at Joachim with blue eyes that were crystal clear and filled with sorrow. His heart tripped in his chest, making him want to move even closer.

"I never should have left your house," she said, seemingly oblivious to the way her nearness affected him. "It wasn't because of any distrust for you or your sister. It was me. I didn't want to cause you any problems. If Victor found me at your house, I'm not sure what he would have done. Plus, I need to get to Willkommen. My sister Miriam—"

She shook her head. "I haven't mentioned my aunt. My sister, my mother and I came here to find her, but dirty cops hijacked our car. Miriam and I were taken and our mother was killed. Victor said he bought me so I could take care of his mother. I'm still so confused." She pulled in a ragged breath. "It was crazy of me to think I could have found my way to Willkommen, yet it seemed like the best choice I had in that moment. I don't have any place else to go."

"You have my house. Victor will not find you there. I will protect you."

At least Joachim hoped he could keep her safe. "Willkommen is a two-hour buggy ride from Petersville," he tried to explain. "Even if you were strong, the trip would be difficult for you to manage on foot. You have been held captive. You must gain your strength first. I will take you when you are ready."

"I wasn't thinking." Sarah tugged at a strand of her golden hair. "Or maybe I was thinking too much about getting away from Victor."

Joachim held out his hand. She placed hers in his, her touch light, but she was trembling and her pale face gave him even more cause for concern. She needed time to rest and gain her strength. Good food and lots of sleep would help build up Sarah's reserve. Then they could think about traveling to Willkommen.

"Rebecca will wonder where we are," he said. "We will go now and take a path that leads through the woods. The spot where we will cross the road is thick with trees on both sides of the pavement. We will move slowly and keep watch lest Victor be close at hand."

"I'm all right, Joachim. You don't have to worry about me."

But he *was* worried. He was worried about the fatigue written so plainly across her sweet face. She was too thin and too pale, and no matter how strong she tried to appear, she needed rest and nourishment.

He had to get Sarah to his house to keep her safe. Hopefully, she wouldn't run away again because next time he might not be able to save her.

Once they arrived back at the Burkholder house, Joachim held the kitchen door open for Sarah and motioned her inside.

"Rebecca has lunch ready," he said, as they stepped over the threshold and into the warmth of the Amish home. "A good meal is what we both need."

His eyes were filled with understanding as he looked at her and smiled. "Is that not right?"

"I am hungry," Sarah admitted, grateful for Joachim's focus on food instead of mentioning her foolish mistake of thinking she could outwit Victor.

Just as Joachim had mentioned, she needed to gain strength before she journeyed to Willkommen. Besides, Victor said Miriam might be arriving at his house in a day or two. This wasn't the time for Sarah to run scared.

"Joachim, you are ready for a cup of coffee?" Rebecca asked as she entered the kitchen, her needlework still in her hands. From her casual gait and nonchalance, she evidently had not realized what had transpired after Sarah left the house.

*"Yah,"* Joachim said with a nod. "I will wash my hands, and then I will also be ready for the meats and cheeses you have placed on the table."

He and Sarah both washed at the sink. Rebecca filled mugs with coffee and motioned Sarah to sit next to her at the table.

Joachim sat across from both women and bowed his head.

Sarah and Rebecca followed suit, with each person praying silently.

*Thank You, Lord,* Sarah mentally intoned, *for Joachim rescuing me in the woods, and thank You for providing this place of shelter from the storm. Send Miriam and let me help her escape whoever is holding her captive so she and I can be together again.*

She glanced up to find Joachim staring at her. Her chest tightened, and a warmth tingled her neck. Glancing away, she reached for the meats and cheeses and placed a slice of each on a piece of bread.

Hungry though she was, Sarah kept thinking of Victor's mother, knowing Ms. Hazel was at the mercy of her son. What would become of the frail woman if Victor left the area for good?

"You are thinking of Victor?" Joachim asked.

"His mother. She's bedridden. A sweet lady who is too infirm to help herself."

"Victor is not to be trusted." Rebecca said with a decisive nod.

Sarah reached for her coffee, not willing to let her expression reveal her own struggle, knowing she had wanted to believe Victor when he'd first taken her from the cabin where she and Miriam had been held. He had told her he would keep her safe from the men who planned to traffic both sisters across state lines. Had it been the drugs that made Sarah believe—at least for a day or two—that he would protect her?

Joachim placed his mug on the table and cocked his head. "A vehicle approaches."

Sarah recognized the sound. Her stomach tightened, and she clutched her hands. "What if it's Victor?"

"Stay inside." Joachim left the table. "Do not let anyone see you."

He opened the door and stepped onto the porch. Rebecca ran to open the window over the sink.

"It is a pickup truck," she relayed to Sarah. "A man is driving. Red hair."

She glanced back at Sarah. "*Yah*, it is Victor."

Sarah wanted to find a closet and hide.

"The pantry." Rebecca pointed to the walk-in alcove. "He will not see you there."

Sarah's heart nearly pounded out of her chest. She hurried into the pantry. Peering around the curtain that divided the cupboard area from the kitchen, she watched the truck pull to a stop.

"Hey, Amish." Victor's raised voice floated through the partially open window. "I spotted the woman I told you about. She disappeared in the woods. If you see her, let me know."

"Why do you need to find this woman?" Joachim asked, his voice calm and rational in contrast to Victor's nervous high pitch.

"Sarah worked for my mother. Now she's gone. In fact, if you know of an Amish girl who wants a job, I need to hire someone."

"Dependable help is hard to find," Joachim said.

"As sickly as my mother has become, I doubt she'll live long. I plan to get the house ready to sell. Come over tomorrow. I have work for you, and remember to let me know if you see that woman."

Victor turned his truck around and drove off.

Sarah's heart hammered in her chest. If she had been outside on the porch, or even standing next to a window, Victor would have spotted her.

Joachim entered the kitchen and hurried to where she stood, her eyes wide and back to the wall.

"He is gone," Joachim assured her.

Sarah was too frightened to move. Victor had found her once. He could find her again no matter what Joachim did to try to stop him.

Fear. Joachim had seen it in Sarah's pretty blue eyes when he had come back inside the house after Victor had driven away.

"He is gone," Joachim assured her again. From the look on her face, he knew his words did little to quell her upset.

A knock sounded at the front door. Sarah took a step back and gasped.

Joachim glanced at Rebecca. "You are expecting someone?"

"Levi Plank has been helping me while *Mamm* and *Datt* are away." She peered from the kitchen window. "*Yah*, it is Levi."

Her voice took on a lilt Joachim had not heard, and the blush to her cheeks made him pause.

"Levi is a friend," Rebecca assured Sarah. "You do not need to be afraid."

But her words did little to change the concern written so plainly on Sarah's face. She backed even farther into the pantry and covered her mouth with her hand; all the while her eyes sought out Joachim. He nodded his encouragement before he stepped toward the door.

Years before, the young Amish man had been his brother Eli's friend. Both the same age, Levi had been the quiet, pensive one whose personality contrasted sharply with Eli's charisma.

Rebecca opened the door, her eyes twinkling with interest, a warm and welcoming smile on her face as she invited Levi inside. "I have a surprise that I did not expect. Joachim has come home."

In the five years that Joachim had been away, the quiet youth had grown into a muscular man whose grip was strong and firm when the two men shook hands.

"This is a *gut* surprise," Levi said. Then as if overcome with enthusiasm, he pulled Joachim close and slapped his back. "You have been missed."

The sincerity of his welcome touched Joachim. "It is good to see you, my friend."

"Our parting was difficult. I trust you have been well. It was time for you to come home, *yah*?"

Joachim nodded. "It was time."

Levi's gaze turned to the alcove where Sarah peered with wide eyes at the gathering.

"You have brought someone home with you?" Levi asked, a hint of confusion evident in his tone.

Sarah took a step forward as Joachim introduced her to Levi. "Sarah needed a place to stay," Rebecca quickly volunteered. "She will remain with us for a day or two."

"You have found a good house," Levi said with a nod. "Plus, Rebecca is known for her pies and cakes."

He rubbed his stomach. "Often she asks me to taste her baked items after the chores." He smiled at the young Amish woman. "Perhaps today we will all be able to enjoy a slice or two of pie."

Rebecca laughed. "*Yah*, that is possible after the animals are watered and fed. You know I cannot resist you, Levi, with all the help you have provided."

"Then I will hurry to the chores as my mouth waters for the special treat that awaits."

Joachim nodded. "I, too, am grateful for your help, Levi. We will go together."

"I will bake something while you both work," Rebecca assured them. She glanced at Sarah. "We will both remain in the house and watch for Victor."

"Victor Thomin?" Levi asked.

*"Yah."* Rebecca nodded. "He is a dangerous man. I do not know how Naomi could work so long in his house."

"My sister helped Ms. Hazel, but she had nothing to do with Victor. Ms. Hazel lived alone back then."

Sarah stepped from the alcove. "Your sister was the Amish woman Ms. Hazel mentioned? She misses Naomi."

"We all miss her," Levi admitted.

"I don't understand," Sarah said.

Levi pursed his lips and thought for a moment before responding. "Victor came home. She did not like being around him, but we fear something else could have happened because she left not only the job but also the area. We have not heard from Naomi since then."

Sarah's brow furrowed. "Did you go to the police?"

"The Amish in this community do not trust the Petersville police. It is commonly known that they can be bribed and bought. My *datt* would not have gone to them, except for his concern for Naomi's welfare." Levi's voice took on an angry edge as he continued. "They were no help and said Naomi must have left for a better life among the *Englisch*."

Rebecca patted his shoulder, offering support.

He nodded his thanks and then continued. "It was not

what my father wanted to hear. We will not go to the police again. They do not understand our ways. Some say they are only interested in their own gain."

"Victor told me the police were corrupt," Sarah shared. "Although he is corrupt as well, so I don't know if I can believe what he said. Still, my sister's car was hijacked by men claiming to be police." She quickly explained being sold to Victor and how Joachim had helped her escape today.

Levi was right, Joachim thought. The Amish did not trust the police, but Victor needed to be stopped by law enforcement. Perhaps Sarah would change her mind about notifying the authorities if she knew them to be honorable. Right now, she was exhausted and still traumatized by what had happened. Joachim would broach the subject again later. In the meantime he would do everything possible to keep her safe.

# FIVE

Sarah appreciated the bath Rebecca drew while the men worked outdoors. The fragrance of the sweet-smelling soap she provided filled the air like a spring bouquet. Sarah stepped from the tub feeling rejuvenated and grateful as she slipped into the Amish dress Rebecca had provided.

"With a clean body, you must also have fresh clothes," Rebecca stated as she instructed Sarah on how to pin the fabric and then adjust the apron around her waist.

"What about the bonnet?" Sarah asked.

"It is a prayer *kapp*. Amish women cover their heads when they pray."

"But you wear it all the time?"

"This is true. We are always ready to pray when our head is covered."

"I pray but perhaps not often enough," Sarah admitted.

"The *kapp* will remind you to do so."

Sarah thought of being in the closet as a child. The smoke had seeped under the door, making her even more afraid. God hadn't saved her even though Sarah had prayed. Thankfully, Miriam had come to her rescue.

"Did you ever pray for something that didn't come about so that you felt God refused your prayer?" Sarah asked.

"*Gott* does not refuse prayer, but sometimes that which we desire is not according to His will." Rebecca sighed. "I told you that Joachim and I had a younger brother named Eli, who died in a buggy accident. My *mamm* prayed for him to live."

"I'm so sorry about your brother."

"As I mentioned earlier, it was *Gott*'s will." Rebecca smiled ruefully. "This is what my *mamm* believes."

"And your father?"

Rebecca's face clouded. "My father does not blame *Gott*." She hesitated as if weighing whether to say something else, then shrugging, she added, "He blames Joachim."

Before Sarah could question her further, Rebecca picked up the white bonnet from where she had placed it on the dresser and handed it to Sarah. Earlier, she had pulled her towel-dried hair into a bun, and she now placed the bonnet on her head.

Rebecca stood back and nodded her approval. "You look like an Amish woman. Victor will not recognize you if he returns to talk to Joachim."

Sarah's stomach roiled thinking again of the hateful man who had held her against her will for too long. How could his mother, who seemed sweet and unassuming, birth a baby who would grow to be so vicious?

What had caused Victor to turn out so bad? She shook her head at the issues within families. Sarah's oldest sister, Hannah, had left three years ago. Sarah had pleaded for her to stay, but Hannah said she had to leave. Sarah hadn't understood her reasoning or why Hannah had never contacted them again.

When she begged her mother to reach out to Hannah and ask her to return home, her mother had shoved the request aside, just as she ignored anything that didn't suit her. Sarah never understood how she could turn her back on her own child. Although too many times her mother had turned her back on Miriam and Sarah. At least Sarah had always had Miriam, but where was she now and would the two women ever be reunited?

The rain returned. Fat drops pounded the barnyard, and thunder rumbled overhead. Joachim and Levi hurried to finish the chores.

Glancing at the upstairs window, Joachim thought of when he had first seen Sarah. Had it been only a few hours since their eyes had connected at the Thomin home?

He followed Levi into the barn. The two men spoke little as they worked, but the silence was comfortable, and the physical labor relaxed the tension in Joachim's shoulders. Some of his earlier concern about Sarah evaporated, and instead of confusion, he felt a sense of purpose and right order.

"Your father is a *gut* farmer, but he is getting old," Levi confided as he paused for a moment to wipe his brow.

"*Datt* planned for Eli and me to work the land with him," Joachim admitted. "Now he needs to find help. You are good to aid him, Levi."

"I help only when he is not in town. He is too proud to take on another person the rest of the time."

Joachim nodded. "*Yah*, he is proud."

"He will be glad to see you."

"You are good to give me comfort by your hopeful words, but I do not think my *datt* will welcome me home."

Levi narrowed his gaze. "You come asking forgiveness, *yah*?"

"I do, but my father and I must both bridge the divide between us. I will walk halfway. I hope he will walk halfway, as well."

"Sometimes the son must walk farther, especially if the father believes he is right."

Joachim pondered Levi's words while he added feed to the troughs and watched the horses eat the newly offered grain.

Levi might think his father would be open to Joachim coming home, but what if his homecoming brought back too many memories of what had happened? Maybe when he faced his father again, Joachim would discover that he had been foolish to think reconciliation was possible.

Once the horses were fed, the two men rolled up their sleeves and washed their hands and arms at the water pump, and then ran to the house as lightning split the sky.

Joachim opened the door and hurried into the kitchen ahead of Levi.

Rebecca stood at the stove, holding a pie that she had just pulled from the oven.

"The storm comes again," he said as he crossed the kitchen to the towel hanging on a hook.

He dried his hands, then glanced up as Rebecca turned to face him. His heart lurched in his chest, sending a new wave of confusion over him. He stared openmouthed at the Amish woman.

Not Rebecca. The face he saw beneath the white *kapp* made his breath catch in his throat.

*Sarah.*

"Rebecca provided the clothes." Sarah's hand wrapped through the fabric of the skirt. "Your sister said Victor would not recognize me like this."

"My sister is right." Joachim struggled to find his voice. "I did not recognize you at first glance."

"You think I look like Rebecca?"

Her blue eyes reached into his heart. She was beautiful. Not because she was in the Amish dress or because her hair was pulled into a bun but because some of the pain she had worn earlier had eased. The lines that tugged at her face had lifted, and the open honesty of her gaze hit him anew.

"Joachim, you haven't answered me," she said, her eyes filled with concern. "Is something wrong?"

"Nothing is wrong and you do not look like Rebecca, but I am surprised to see you as an Amish woman."

"Am I offending you?"

He shook his head. "You could never offend me."

Levi hurried inside and stopped by the door to wipe his feet. Bewilderment washed over his face as he glanced first at Sarah and then at Rebecca, who stepped back into the kitchen.

"You are both staring as if you have never seen a woman in an Amish dress," Rebecca said with a laugh.

Levi pointed to the stove. "I was wondering if you could spare a cup of coffee and a slice of pie for a hungry man."

"*Yah*, of course." Rebecca's cheeks glowed with a hint of embarrassment. "But I have ham and cheese on the table, along with fresh baked bread. You need to eat something substantial before you have your pie."

Levi smiled as he accepted the cup of coffee she offered. "You know what I need even before I do."

The twinkle in her eyes warmed Joachim's heart. Rebecca's interest in the young man was more than evident, and Levi seemed taken with her, as well. Joachim was happy for his *schweschder* and hoped Levi would start the courting process soon. Perhaps Joachim could chaperone and take them for rides in the country. He would occupy his mind with thoughts of pretty Sarah in her blue dress and white apron while Rebecca and Levi chatted with each other.

If only Sarah was wearing the Amish dress as a woman of their faith instead of as an *Englischer* who needed to hide her identity and had nothing else to wear.

Joachim and Sarah sipped coffee as Levi ate the lunch Rebecca had provided. Although Sarah said little, her eyes took in the conversation he and Levi had about the farm and what could be done if his *datt* were open to accepting help to make the fields more productive.

"The Amish Market in Willkommen is a fine place to sell produce and baked goods," Levi shared. "My uncle goes twice a week as do many of the other Amish farmers. The *Englisch* come from as far away as Atlanta. They buy handcrafted items, too—including woodwork. You could do well in this area, Joachim, if you opened a shop in town."

He shook his head and laughed. "I am a carpenter, Levi, not a store clerk."

"Yet you charge for your labor when you go house to house. How different would that be from selling chairs and tables and lawn furniture to walk-in customers?"

Although Levi had a point, Joachim saw only the folly in his comment. Once his father returned home and Joachim had a chance to talk to his parents, he doubted they would want him to remain at home. In fact, Rebecca would probably be chastised for allowing Joachim to stay in the house while their parents were out of town. There would be no point in Joachim staying in the area and opening a shop if he was shunned by his family.

Suddenly, his mood dampened, and the coffee tasted bitter in his mouth.

"You will have pie?" Sarah asked as she and Rebecca cleared the table once Levi had eaten.

Joachim nodded. "Only a small slice. There is much yet to be done. The fences need repair. The barn, as well. Tomorrow I will go to Victor's house. Today, I will work here."

"I'm sure your father will appreciate your help."

If only that would be so, yet Joachim suspected his *datt* would be hard-pressed to appreciate anything his son did.

Sarah accepted a small piece of pie from Rebecca and carried it to table.

*"Denki,"* Joachim said as he took the plate from her.

She glanced at Levi. "I'm sure you would like pie."

"*Yah*, but a much larger slice than Joachim," the younger man said with a grin. He glanced at Joachim. "I must work for my father this afternoon, and tomorrow is the barn raising. Did Rebecca tell you?"

Joachim shook his head.

"The Byler barn burned," Levi continued. "Samuel had wood delivered, and he has asked us to arrive in the morning. We could use your help, Joachim."

"Of course. Samuel is a *gut* man. If he needs help, I will be there."

As Joachim and Levi ate the pie, Rebecca wrapped cheesecloth around a second pie and tied the edges together. "I baked extra for your *mamm*. Tell her thank-you for the onions she sent yesterday. They were sweet and will keep in the root cellar."

Levi smiled. "She will like to hear that her gift was well received."

"*Yah*, of course, it was."

"She always asks about you, Rebecca. You should come to visit."

"Perhaps when *Mamm* and *Datt* return."

"They will not be gone much longer?" Joachim posed.

"Only a few more days," Rebecca responded. "But, Levi, I will see your *mamm* tomorrow at the barn raising. She will be there, *yah*?"

"Probably not. Her arthritis is bad, especially when it rains."

Levi bid Joachim and Sarah farewell and accepted the

pie from Rebecca. She walked outside with him, and the couple stood talking on the porch.

Joachim glanced at Sarah. She rinsed dishes in a bucket of water at the sink. "You will be all right here in the house with Rebecca if I am working in the barn?" he asked.

"Of course, I'll be fine. Don't worry."

"I was not worried."

"Then you were concerned."

"Perhaps," he said with a shrug. "I know you were frightened when Victor drove onto the property earlier."

"You should tell him to stay off your land."

"*Yah*, this I could do. But that is not how a good neighbor acts."

She narrowed her gaze. "Is it necessary to be a good neighbor to a man who is so hateful?"

"If I want him to think I have nothing against him." Before he could explain what he meant, the back door opened and Rebecca returned to the kitchen.

"I am interrupting something?" she asked.

"No," Sarah insisted. "But I am tired and would like to rest."

Joachim peered through the window at the darkening sky. "Black clouds roll overhead. The storm may turn the day to night. Perhaps you will need a candle in your room."

Sarah's face tightened. She shook her head. "There's still plenty of daylight. Besides, I don't like candles."

Joachim didn't understand her comment, nor did he understand the fear that returned to her face and the way she clasped her hands together. Something about candles had set her off, but what? And why?

"Perhaps the oil lamp would be better," Rebecca offered.

"I'll be fine," Sarah insisted. "The room has a window. I will awake before nightfall, if I can even sleep."

Sarah grabbed her skirts and hurried upstairs. Her footfalls echoed in the house and made Joachim's heart ache.

He had to let her go, but he wondered what the *Englischer* was hiding. Sarah feared Victor, but there was something else she feared.

# SIX

Sarah hadn't realized how exhausted she was until she removed the bonnet and apron and lay on the bed. She draped the quilt over her legs and turned her head away from the diffused light coming from the windows. In less than a minute, she was sound asleep.

Sometime later, a noise startled her awake. She turned to glance out the window, seeing the failing light. The steady rhythmic pitter-patter of raindrops on the roof made her want to close her eyes again.

She began to drift back into a light slumber when someone pounded on the downstairs door. She sat up, slipped her feet into her shoes and hurried to the window. She peered around the curtain, but all she could see was the barn, not the drive where a car or buggy, undoubtedly, sat parked.

Not a red pickup truck.

But what if it was Victor?

Her breath caught in her throat as the banging started again.

Where were Joachim and Rebecca?

And what if the person at the door *was* Victor?

Sarah's hand rose to her throat. She glanced around the room, searching for a closet in which to hide, but the Amish bedroom had no closets and only one door that led to the hallway. She backed into the corner beyond the bed, as far as she could get from the window, her pulse racing.

She spied the prayer *kapp* on the dresser where she had placed it. Rebecca's mention of an Amish woman always being prepared to pray circled through her mind.

"Lord, he-help me," she stuttered. The words stuck in her throat.

A voice sounded outside. Joachim's voice.

Slowly, she approached the window, making sure she was not visible from below.

Joachim stood at the doorway of the barn talking to someone. Her stomach churned. She rubbed her hand across the waistband of her dress, hoping to calm her internal unrest, all the while she silently beseeched Joachim not to reveal her whereabouts if he was talking to Victor.

A sinking feeling settled over her. If she'd trusted the wrong man and Joachim and Victor were actually friends, she could end up back in the attic, being held under lock and key, which was the last thing she wanted.

"Help me, Lord," she mumbled as she tied the apron around her waist, settled the bonnet onto her head and hurried downstairs in hopes of seeing for herself who had come knocking at the door.

Joachim did not expect to be just as broadsided when he saw Sarah for the second time dressed in Amish clothing. Maybe it was her flushed cheeks or the question he read in her gaze that made him stop as he entered the kitchen and stared at her until she seemed ready to flee up the stairs again.

"Who was at the door?" she asked, her eyes hooded. "I heard knocking. It was Victor, wasn't it?"

"It was a man from town who came to buy fresh eggs. He has come often in the past and did not realize Rebecca had taken down the sign about having eggs and baked goods for sale. I told him none were for sale today."

"But—" She shook her head.

"But you thought it was Victor," Joachim said.

"I don't know what I thought. The pounding woke me. I couldn't see the drive—"

"I told you I would keep you safe." But she had not believed him. Joachim let out a frustrated breath, knowing too well that Sarah's trust would be hard earned.

"You're going to his house tomorrow," she said as if to justify the assumption she had incorrectly made.

"I need the work, Sarah. Plus, what better way to keep my eye on Victor? He held you against your will. What if he does the same thing to the next woman he brings home to care for his mother? The police need to be notified so he can be stopped from hurting anyone else."

"No." Her voice was firm. "The police are already too involved."

"Involved in capturing you?"

She turned her back on him and hung her head.

Joachim mentally chastised himself. He had caused her upset, which was the last thing he wanted. "I do not understand," he finally admitted. "Perhaps you can explain everything."

She stepped toward the kitchen table and slipped into a chair. Her face was tight with emotion.

"It is difficult to talk about, *yah*?" he said, following her to the table and sitting across from her.

She offered him a weak smile as if to acknowledge what he said was true. "Until recently, my sister Miriam and I lived outside Knoxville with our mother. She had shown signs of dementia over the last year or so. A few months ago, she started talking about a long-lost sister with whom she wanted to reconnect. Her name is Annie

Miller." Sarah stared at him expectantly. "I believe my aunt lives in Willkommen."

Joachim nodded. "The next town."

"A road sign said it is thirty miles from here."

"*Yah*, that is right."

"On the way to find my aunt, we got lost. It was night. A police car pulled us over. At first I was relieved, thinking they would help us, but then—"

She clasped her hands and held them tight against her heart.

"Something happened," he prompted, knowing the retelling must be difficult.

"There were two police officers, although I wonder if they truly were law enforcement. One of them grabbed Miriam and pulled her from the car. My mother became agitated and opened the passenger door. She wanted to protect my sister, but a second man—he was in the police car."

She hung her head and blinked back tears that filled her eyes. Joachim reached for her hand.

"I can't remember everything, but a second man—the one in the police car—shot my mother."

Joachim hadn't expected her comment. "*Gott* help you, Sarah, for what you had to endure."

"They took Miriam and me to a cabin and held us in separate rooms. Everything after that was a blur. Victor hauled me away at some point. I know he forced me to take drugs that he said would help me. I stashed them in the corner of my mouth and spit them out whenever I could. But I couldn't get rid of all of them. I was in a drugged stupor for too long. Eventually he took me to his mother's home. All told, he held me against my will for two months. When I saw your buggy, I knew I needed to get away. I hadn't taken the pills he offered for a few days so I was clearheaded and able to think for myself." She glanced up at Joachim. "You came at the right time."

Joachim had been drawn home for some reason. He had thought it was to reconcile with his father. Maybe it was because of Sarah's need.

"Now," she continued, "I'm not sure what I should do. Perhaps I should leave."

"Leave?" Had he or his sister done something to upset her? "Surely Rebecca said nothing that caused you concern."

"No, Joachim, your sister has been very helpful and welcoming."

"Then you think I do not want you here? That is not true."

"Victor is your neighbor. Perhaps he's a friend, although I cannot see how you would want anything to do with such a hateful man." She glanced down at the dress she wore. "You were kind to invite me to stay, and I'm grateful for the clean clothing Rebecca has provided. I'll remain here tonight and leave in the morning."

Joachim could not believe what she was saying. The fact that she thought he would have anything to do with Victor was unsettling.

"Victor is not the type of man I would ever call friend. It troubles me, Sarah, to have you think that I would not see with clear vision who he really is. But you have been through so much, and often our minds jump to incorrect conclusions."

His own father had done exactly that. "I told Victor I would start work tomorrow, not because I like the man but because I want to ensure Victor does not cause more harm. When I work at his house, I can see what he is doing and hopefully keep him from harming any other woman.

Plus, you were concerned about his mother. I am, as well. I will find a way to check on her."

Sarah stared at him for a long moment. "I want to trust you, Joachim."

He took her hand. "And you can. If I was a friend to Victor, I would have told him where to find you. He never would have left my father's farm alone if he thought you were here."

She sighed as if weighing his words. "I want to believe you."

"Then *do* believe me, Sarah. It is that easy. You are safe here. Victor will not enter this house, I will make certain of that. You must decide what you want to do and where you want to go. If you want to go to Willkommen, I will take you, but that would be in a few days. First you must get stronger."

Sarah had been held captive for too long. Rebecca's cooking and the peace that even Joachim could feel in the Amish house would replenish Sarah's strength and her health.

That night when they sat at the table, Sarah had little to eat, and the sadness in her eyes worried him even more than her hesitancy to enter into a conversation.

After they finished eating, she started to clear the dishes, but Joachim took her hand. "I will help Rebecca. You need to rest."

"Joachim is right," Rebecca encouraged. "You do not need to help me tonight. You need to sleep."

"But—"

Joachim took her plate and placed it near the sink. "It is dark. You'll need a candle to go upstairs."

Her eyes widened, and she shook her head. "I don't want a candle."

"Perhaps the gas lamp then. You can adjust the wick so

only a small flame will light the room all night if you do not want to remain in the dark."

"The dark doesn't frighten me," she insisted.

But something frightened her.

"I have a flashlight in my buggy. Wait here and I will get it."

"You are Amish, yet you can use a flashlight?"

Rebecca nodded. "We do not run electric wiring into our homes, but flashlights, which are battery powered, are allowed."

Joachim hurried outside and returned soon thereafter with a flashlight in hand. He turned it on. "You will be safe tonight."

She took the flashlight and nodded. "Thank you, Joachim."

Glancing at Rebecca, she added, "Thank you for dinner. Don't let me sleep too late in the morning."

Joachim watched as Sarah slowly climbed the stairs, her footsteps heavy as if she had little or no energy. Would she be able to get over the pain she had experienced?

He thought of her future and wondered where she would go once she gained her strength. To Willkommen to find her aunt and perhaps track down her sister? Or farther away where Joachim would never be able to see her again?

She was *Englisch*. He was Amish.

Whether he liked it or not, the two could never mix.

# SEVEN

Sarah woke the next morning to the smell of bacon and eggs. Her mouth watered, making her realize how hungry she was. Last night with Joachim sitting across the table from her, she had eaten little. Thankfully, she had slept well and now hurried to dress and go downstairs.

Rebecca was clearing the table and turned as Sarah entered the kitchen. "What is wrong this morning? You look worried."

Sarah glanced around the room, seeing the empty skillet on the wood-burning stove. Dirty dishes were piled in the sink, and the butter and jelly sat on the counter.

"I missed breakfast?" *And Joachim*, she wanted to add.

Rebecca motioned her toward the table. "I have kept a plate of bacon warm in the oven. Your place is still set at the table, and eggs will not take long to fry. I can toast the bread or you can eat it as is."

"Thank you, Rebecca, but I hate for you to go to all that trouble."

"It is no trouble. Joachim has already eaten."

Sarah stepped to the window and peered toward the barn. "Is he hitching the horse to the buggy?"

"He is in the east pasture, repairing a fence. One of our cows got out. Thankfully, he got her back, but now he must fix the breach."

Sarah felt a sinking in her stomach. The nervousness she had felt last night returned, and her appetite left her. "Maybe I don't need breakfast."

"You must start the day with food," Rebecca insisted. "I will fetch more eggs from the chicken house."

"Let me. It's the least I can do."

"If you insist." Rebecca handed her a basket. "The nests are just inside the coop. You will see them. There should be plenty of eggs."

Sarah hurried outside, relieved to be of help, and inhaled the fresh country air, enjoying the sense of freedom with the open spaces all around her. For too long, she had been locked in the old Thomin house, which smelled of dust and mildew.

She looked for Joachim, but couldn't see him. She did, however, see a barking dog, which ran from one of the fields, wagging his tail and warming her heart. She bent to pat his head and scratch under his neck. "Aren't you a cute Yorkshire terrier. I'll have to ask Rebecca your name. I'm glad you want to be friends."

The dog licked her hand. "You're what Victor needs. Did you know your ancestors were bred to hunt rats?"

The playful terrier wiggled all the more. His antics made her laugh, which she hadn't done in so long. Even before Victor she couldn't remember the feeling of acceptance that flowed over her with the playful dog so eager for her attention.

She laughed again as the dog danced at her feet. "I need to get the eggs before Rebecca comes looking for me." Sarah scratched the dog's head and then hurried to the hen house with the pup scampering along beside her.

"Don't scare the hens," she warned playfully.

The clucking coming from the hen house assured her she would find eggs, which she quickly did. After filling the small basket Rebecca had given her, Sarah started back to the house.

The sound of a vehicle caused her to turn toward the main road. Her heart stopped.

A car sped by going much too fast. A tan sedan.

She let out the breath she had been holding and hurried to the porch, the pup at her feet.

Rebecca met her at the door, holding a large bag of dog food in one hand. "I see you have met Angelo. He is lovable, *yah*? Maybe too much so at times."

"Angelo?" Sarah smiled down at the dog. "That doesn't sound like an Amish name."

Rebecca chuckled. "He belonged to a local man named DeCaro. When he moved away, he could not take Angelo so we agreed to keep him. The dog is a wanderer. He visits lots of farms and comes back when he's hungry."

She handed Sarah the bag. "We will make a trade. I will begin cooking your eggs if you fill Angelo's bowls. You will find his dishes at the side of the porch."

Sarah enjoyed being useful, and Angelo seemed to appreciate the attention she showered on him as she filled his food dish and a second bowl with fresh water.

Hurrying back inside, she ate the eggs Rebecca had prepared along with the crisp bacon and a thick slice of bread slathered with butter.

"I'm so full," Sarah admitted. "Breakfast was delicious." She stood and carried her empty plate to the sink.

A buggy turned onto the drive. Rebecca hurried to the window and peered outside. "It is Levi. He will take us to the barn raising."

"What about Joachim?" Sarah asked, feeling a knot form in her stomach.

"He will join us later at the Byler home."

"I'll wait for him here."

"Joachim did not want you alone in the house, Sarah. You are to go with us."

"But what if we pass Victor on the road?"

Rebecca smiled. "You will sit in the back of the buggy. Victor will not see you there. Besides, being dressed as an Amish woman protects you from Victor even if he still searches the area. He would not think to look for you among us, and he would not be able to spot you just from passing the barn. The women work in the kitchen getting the lunch ready. He might drive by on the road, but he will not come into the Amish home."

Sarah bit her lip, trying to weigh the pros and cons of leaving the protection of Joachim's home. She had made an almost disastrous mistake by leaving yesterday and didn't want to repeat her error.

"What about the other women?" she asked. "They'll realize I'm not Amish and Victor might find out."

"*Ach*, this is not something that should cause you worry. After what happened with Naomi, the Amish give Victor a wide birth. His true self is known and not admired, to say the least. The Amish ladies you will meet today will not talk to Victor, of this you can be certain."

"But won't they ask questions about where I came from and why I'm with you?"

"We will tell them the truth. You are visiting from Tennessee. We will not mention anything more. You are used to *Englischer* gatherings where perhaps people are inquisitive. The Amish do not pry." She tilted her head. Her eyes twinkled. "At least most of us try not to pry, but there are busybodies even among the Amish. I will make certain you stay away from anyone like this today."

Sarah had to smile at Rebecca's insights. Human nature was human nature no matter the culture. Some people thrived on knowing everything about everyone else.

"You're sure Joachim will join us later?" she asked again.

"*Yah*, I am certain." Rebecca picked up a basket from the table and handed it to Sarah. "Carry this potato salad to the buggy. Levi will tuck it in the rear where it will not turn over. I will bring the pies."

Sarah pulled in a fortifying breath and grabbed the wicker basket. "Did you make the basket?"

"*Yah*, I did. In the winter I weave, and sell my baskets in the warm weather along with the produce from the garden, fresh eggs and my baked items to the people from town."

She handed Sarah a black bonnet with a wide bill, and a lightweight black cape. Once both women were properly attired, they grabbed the baskets and hurried outside to where Levi waited with the buggy.

He arranged the food in the rear and then helped Sarah onto the back seat. Rebecca sat in front next to him.

Sarah peered from the buggy, hoping she was hidden from roving eyes, especially if Victor happened by. She rubbed her right hand over her stomach to still the unrest within her. If only Joachim were at her side.

Levi flicked the reins, and his mare headed to the road. Thankfully, both directions were clear. Sarah settled back in the seat, soothed by the side-to-side sway of the buggy and the clip-clop of the horse's hooves on the pavement as Levi turned the mare onto the main road.

The crisp morning air mixed with the musky scent of the still-damp earth. She turned her gaze to the distant pastures, hoping to catch sight of Joachim. All she saw were a few horses on the hillside and newly tilled fields waiting for planting.

The repetitive cycle of tilling, planting, harvesting year after year had to bring satisfaction to the farmers who worked the soil and depended on God's providence to provide an abundant harvest.

Thinking back on her own life, she saw little fruit, no matter how hard she worked to be productive. She had tried to be a dutiful daughter and sought ways to help her mother, although her efforts always fell short of her mother's expectations. Yet she had continued to try to prove herself.

It had started with the fire that was never talked about, never forgiven. Outrage from her mother would have been better than the silence. At least then the issue could have been discussed and resolved. Instead, it remained a gaping hole in their relationship. A hole that never closed and always festered.

"You are all right?" Rebecca turned to ask, probably hearing another of Sarah's sighs.

"I'm fine. The air is refreshing and the scenery is so picturesque. I'm glad you invited me to join you today."

"We will be there soon. The barn is to be built on the Byler land. As you probably heard Levi mention yesterday, Samuel and Ester lost their barn in a recent fire."

Sarah tugged the cape tight around her neck, trying to push aside the memories from the past.

"Did…did a candle overturn?" she finally asked.

"Lightning caused the fire," Rebecca shared.

"I'm sorry."

"*Yah*, but it is a reason to gather today. The men will work to build the barn, and the women will work in the kitchen so the men have food when their stomachs grumble."

"My stomach is grumbling now for a slice of your pie," Levi joined in with a laugh.

Rebecca poked his arm playfully and turned back to face the road. Levi leaned a bit closer to her, and Rebecca's laughter carried an even stronger lilt.

Sarah's heart warmed to the attraction between them that was so obvious. For half a second she longed for someone in her own life who could make her laugh and take away the pall that hung across her shoulders.

She was being foolish. Such a relationship was not in her future. Her mother had made mistakes in the men she chose. Sarah had learned wisely to guard her feelings lest she, too, succumb to a man who would break her heart or her spirit. Love was not for everyone. Her mother was proof of that.

The ride to the farm took a little more than twenty minutes. Levi helped Sarah climb down from the buggy and then handed her the same basket she had carried earlier.

A two-story Amish house stood nearby with small outbuildings directly behind the main structure. A stream of women climbed the porch steps and entered the house carrying baskets and bowls and boxes. Sarah imagined the delightful offerings loaded within the containers—cakes and cookies and freshly baked bread.

In the distance, lumber was neatly piled in stacks on the ground. Giant frames lay waiting to be raised. Beyond the location for the new barn, she saw the charred remains of a former structure, now little more than burned rubble. The acrid smell of smoke wafted past her and made her turn from the destruction and focus on the men milling close to the woodpiles. They chatted amicably among themselves, and laughter punctuated their conversation.

Sarah had read somewhere that the barn and house raisings combined neighborly help with social time and were important mainstays of the Amish life. Even as an outsider, she could sense the excitement and an energy that was almost palpable.

Although buoyed by what she saw, thoughts of Victor returned and brought Sarah back to her own predicament.

Longing for the protection of the house, she hurried in that direction, unwilling to be out in the open for long, especially with Joachim nowhere in sight.

Levi joined the other men while Rebecca fell in step next to Sarah.

"The women will know I am not Amish." Sarah repeated her earlier concern. Surrounded by the Amish, she realized how much she stood out, in spite of the clothing she wore. Surely the women would recognize her attempt to be something she wasn't.

"Do not worry," Rebecca said. "I told you before, all you must say is that you are a friend visiting from Tennessee. This is true. You do not need to enter into long conversations with the other women. Just smile and nod."

Which sounded so easy when Rebecca said it, but as Sarah stepped into the house overflowing with women, she felt totally out of place. Following Rebecca's lead, she removed her cape and black bonnet and hung them on a peg by the door.

Lowering her gaze, she walked behind Rebecca into the kitchen and was relieved when someone handed her a whisk and a half-filled mixing bowl.

"The cream needs to be whipped," the woman instructed before she moved to the stove to stir a pot of what looked like homemade noodles.

Complying with the woman's wishes, Sarah stood in the corner, beating the cream with a steady motion. Thankfully, the women were so busy preparing the meal that they paid little attention to the newcomer.

Once the cream was whipped, Sarah helped grate cabbage for the slaw and clean carrots and kale fresh from the Bylers' garden.

The smells of succulent meats and vegetable casseroles, mixed with the warm scent of baked goods, made her look forward to the luncheon in spite of the hearty breakfast she had eaten this morning.

Glancing through the window, she smiled at the young children playing close to the house, watched over by older girls who hauled food to the long tables set up in the shade of the mighty oaks.

"You will help me?" Rebecca asked as she lifted a large container of lemonade from the sink. "We will use a small wagon to take this to the men."

Sarah wiped her hands on a nearby towel and followed Rebecca outside. Together, they pulled the wagon to where the men worked. The frame had been raised while the women were busy in the kitchen. Now the barn had a sturdy outer structure upon which men climbed.

The steady tap of their hammers filled the air, along with the grinding of hand drills and the grating rasp of saws, cutting through the four-by-fours. The smell of fresh wood overpowered the earlier scent of the fire, and Sarah breathed in the clean aroma as she scanned the structure.

Her heart leaped in her chest when she spied Joachim, big and strong, perched high atop the massive support frame. He hammered a crossbeam into place, seemingly oblivious to the danger of being so precariously poised.

"Joachim doesn't fear heights, it seems," she said, her eyes focused on his long legs and strong arms.

Rebecca followed her gaze. "My brother has been a climber since he was a boy. *Yah*, he fears little."

Once the beam was nailed in place, he glanced down, finding Sarah in the swarm of people as if he had eyes only for her.

Her spine tingled and a smile parted her lips. Joachim waved in response, filling her with a sense of well-being.

Rebecca poured lemonade into glasses, and Sarah distributed them to the men who eagerly accepted the refreshing drink.

Grabbing Sarah's arm, Rebecca pointed to the road.

Sarah's breath caught. Victor's pickup pulled into the drive and braked to a stop near the house.

He stepped out and stood for a long moment, staring at the gathering of workers.

Sarah clutched Rebecca's hand in fear. Victor was near the porch, blocking her path to the kitchen. Her pulse raced. Exposed and in danger of being discovered, she searched for a hiding spot.

Her only recourse were the outbuildings. Trying not to be obvious, she wove her way between the men.

A barking dog drew her attention to the open field. Angelo appeared in the distance racing toward her, his tail wagging.

She glanced back. Victor turned in her direction at the same moment. His eyes widened, and he pushed through the children playing on the lawn.

Sarah ran. Skirting the first shed, she edged around a second building to where another structure stood.

If only the door was unlocked. She climbed the stairs, grabbed the knob and pushed on the door, relieved that it opened. Slipping inside, she saw the pile of sawdust in the corner and the various woodworking machines. She pulled in a deep breath and closed the door behind her.

From the window, she caught sight of Victor. He glanced again at the house and then walked with determined steps toward the workshop.

A dog barked. She peered through the window. Angelo stood at the door, demanding entry. Victor rounded the second outbuilding and was heading straight for her.

She climbed behind a pile of plywood.

Her heart pounded. A roar filled her ears. Her pulse

raced so that she was sure the entire workshop must be shaking in sync with her trembling body.

Angelo continued to bark. He wanted to be let in, right now.

Footsteps sounded outside. The door creaked open. She held her breath. Sawdust tickled her nose so that she wanted to sneeze but she managed to stay silent.

"What's going on, you stupid mutt?" Victor demanded, his voice gravelly and laced with anger. "Did someone come in here?"

She envisioned Angelo clawing at the plywood, drawing Victor's attention to where she hid.

If the dog didn't reveal her presence, the unbridled pounding of her heart would alert him for sure.

Angelo barked again.

*Please, Lord.*

"What'd you find, boy?" Victor drew closer. "What's behind that pile of plywood?"

"Is there something you need?" Joachim's voice as he entered the workshop.

Victor growled. "I saw that woman who cared for my mother. She came in here."

Joachim laughed. "You are seeing things unless she is Amish. No *Englischer* is here."

Victor stepped closer to the plywood. Angelo sniffed at the opening to where she huddled.

"The dog's found something, Amish. The woman's hiding."

Something scurried across the floor. Angelo chased after it.

Victor gasped.

"It was only a mouse," Joachim assured him.

Sarah held her breath. Victor hated rats. Hopefully, his dislike of rodents included mice.

"I saw the commotion from the road and wondered if I would find you here. Why aren't you at my house?" Victor groused.

"This morning I must help with the barn. Perhaps you will stay and eat with the Amish? The women have been cooking for days. Later, I will come to your house."

Victor huffed. "I need to go to town this afternoon so don't keep me waiting."

"And the lunch?" Joachim asked.

"I don't want your food." Victor stomped out of the workshop. The door slammed behind him.

"Sarah?" Joachim was moving the wood.

A flurry of fine wood particles filled the air. Then his arms were around her, pulling her from her hiding spot.

"Are you all right?"

"Oh, Joachim." She let out the breath she had been holding. "Victor almost found me. If you hadn't—"

Joachim pulled her closer. "Angelo is the one who saved you by scaring that mouse out of its hiding spot."

"Angleo may have saved me, but he also caused the initial hoopla that drew Victor's attention. By the way, I don't like mice," she admitted, "but anything to keep Victor away."

Rebecca opened the door and peered inside. "He is gone."

Joachim stepped away from Sarah, leaving her feeling vulnerable. She wanted to be back in his arms, but she resisted the urge to move closer.

Why was she letting down her guard around Joachim? Sarah was an *Englisch* woman who had no place in his Amish world.

# EIGHT

Joachim hated the disrepair he found in the Thomin home. Sagging gutters, peeling paint, broken shutters, but the worst problem was the dry rot. When Victor's father, Mr. Thomin, was alive, he had kept the house in tip-top shape. A woodworker by hobby, he had taken pride in ensuring the house was well maintained. The father had died when Victor was a teen. Ms. Hazel had maintained the home until her health started to fail. In her declining years, she struggled to care for the inside of the house and did little for the exterior. Joachim could work on the house for weeks and still not shore up all of the more deep-seated structural problems that would require even more extensive work.

He glanced at the drive and wondered how long Victor would be gone. A niggling voice kept playing Sarah's words in his head, especially her concern for Victor's mother. Joachim needed to check on the elderly woman. He would never forgive himself if something happened to her.

He placed his tools on the porch, wiped his hands on a rag and stamped his feet, not wanting to track dirt into the home. After peering again at the driveway, he reached for the kitchen doorknob.

"Joachim?"

He turned, surprised to see Sarah running toward him

from the path through the woods. Concern clutched his heart.

"What are you doing here? Is something wrong at the farm?" Instantly he regretted the harshness of his tone when he saw the grimace on her face as if she had been offended by his question.

"Did Rebecca send you?" he asked.

She shook her head. "But she told me about the shortcut through the woods. I thought it would be safe to come because Victor said he would be gone this afternoon. I'm worried about my sister. He promised me Miriam would join me either today or tomorrow. I should have mentioned it this morning, but after what happened at the barn raising, I wasn't thinking straight. Did you see anyone? Miriam's tall with brown hair."

"You need to go home, Sarah. Victor left for town, but who knows when he will be back. I was going inside the house to see about Victor's mother when I heard you call my name. I will check on her and see if any other woman is being held inside, but first, you must return to my house."

"No, Joachim. Victor will be gone for a while. I need to see how Ms. Hazel is with my own eyes. Maybe she'll know something about Miriam."

"It is too dangerous," he insisted.

Sarah pushed past him and opened the door.

As frightened as she was of Victor, Sarah seemed determined to see his mother for herself.

"You are making a mistake," he warned.

"Guard the door and let me know if you see Victor."

Joachim shook his head. "You are not going anywhere without me. Besides, we will have a better view of the road from the upstairs window. I will keep watch from there."

Sarah hurried up the stairs, and Joachim followed. At the top of the landing, she tuned left and opened the door to a large bedroom. Mahogany furniture filled the room. Ms. Hazel lay on a king-size bed, looking tiny and frail against the large pillows and down comforter.

Sarah hurried to the bed and touched the woman's arm.

Joachim stepped to the window, relieved that he could see the roadway in the distance and the route Victor would take home.

"She's asleep, and I can't wake her," Sarah said, her voice filled with concern. "Ms. Hazel, can you hear me?"

Finally, the woman groaned. Her eyes fluttered open for a minute, long enough for a sweet smile to cover her lips before she drifted to sleep again.

A tray sat on a small table near the bed with the remains of a piece of toast and a soft-boiled egg. "It looks like she had something to eat not too long ago," Joachim said. "Maybe Victor is taking better care of her than you thought he would."

"If only that were true. He left her alone in this big house."

"I was working outside."

"And would you have heard her cry out if she needed help? Plus, you weren't here this morning when he stopped by the Bylers' farm."

Sarah moved to the dresser, pulled open the top drawer and took out a pill bottle. "The label is made out to Hazel Thomin, but the bottle is empty. It's for Cardoxin, which sounds like it might be a heart medicine. All the while I've been here, Victor has never refilled her prescription."

She pulled out another bottle. "This one has remained empty, too. It's Lasix. Mother took that. It's a diuretic to eliminate fluid buildup within the body."

"Perhaps Victor keeps the filled bottles of pills in his own room."

Sarah flashed him a look of frustration and opened a

second drawer. Her eyes widened as she held up a third bottle. "Over-the-counter sleeping medication. Half the pills are gone."

She looked at Joachim. "Do you know what this means?"

"That Victor needs to refill her medication?"

Sarah frowned. "The sleeping pills are one way to ensure an infirmed woman doesn't try to get out of bed or wander around the house. If Victor is sedating his mother, he's despicable. Even more so than I had initially thought."

Joachim flicked his glance back to the road and his stomach soured. "His truck, Sarah. He is turning into the driveway. Hurry. You must leave the house now."

She returned the pills to the drawers and then raced from the room and down the stairs.

Joachim followed her. On the first floor, she peered through a window. Victor parked his truck and then stepped out of the vehicle onto the driveway with a scowl on his face.

"You have to hide," Joachim warned.

But where?

She opened the door to the basement and scurried down the steps. He closed the door behind her.

"What are you doing?" Victor's voice.

He burst into the kitchen, his eyes filled with fury as if ready to lambast anyone who stood in his way.

Victor stopped short, seeing Joachim at the sink, holding a glass of water to his lips. He drank it down in one large gulp, then smiled at Victor. "I trust you had a good trip?"

"What are you doing inside the house?"

"I did not think you would mind me getting a drink of water. If this is a problem, I will bring a jug of water with me tomorrow."

Victor flicked his gaze around the kitchen as if to make certain nothing was disturbed. "Did you go anywhere else?"

"I told you I needed a drink of water. Is this a problem?"

"No, of course not. Did anyone stop by the house?"

"You are expecting someone, perhaps?"

"No one. I just thought—"

He let the sentence hang.

Joachim pushed past him. "I must return to my work, but first you should see what I found on the opposite side of the house. You have time for me to show you now?"

"More problems that will cost more money?"

"I believe you have spare wood in one of the sheds outside. I saw this, *yah*?"

"My father's shop. You can use anything from there."

"That was my hope." He motioned Victor forward. "Come, let us walk to the front of the house. I will show you the problem."

Joachim had been digging out dry rot all afternoon, never thinking he would be able to use the disrepair as a decoy for Sarah.

He squared his shoulders, knowing he needed to distract Victor long enough for Sarah to escape.

If he only could.

The basement was dank and smelled of mildew. Light from a small window allowed Sarah to make her way down the stairs and then to the far corner of the basement where she stood, listening for any sign of Victor opening the kitchen door and descending to where she hid. She had been foolish to enter the house, even if she'd wanted to ensure Ms. Hazel was all right.

Muffled voices came from the kitchen, followed by footfalls as the two men walked through the house and left through the front door. She hurried to that side of the basement and peered through a mud-splattered window. Joachim was talking to Victor and pointing to the house.

If Joachim could distract Victor long enough, Sarah could leave through the kitchen and pick up the path just beyond the barn.

She started for the stairs and then stopped. A scratching sound came from the other side of the basement. She had little time to waste but paused as the scratching repeated.

Moving even farther into the rear of the basement, Sarah noticed a small alcove and a padlocked door. The scratching came again.

Sarah tapped on the door. The scratching continued.

Her heart stopped. Was someone signaling from behind the door?

She searched for keys to open the locks but found none.

Knowing she had to be careful, she put her mouth to the door and whispered, "My name's Sarah. I'll come back to help you. Can you hear me?"

Silence.

She glanced back at the window. Joachim couldn't keep Victor occupied much longer. Sarah would be of no help to anyone if she fell into Victor's control again.

She hurried up the stairs and slowly opened the kitchen door. The muffled sounds of the men's voices filtered through the house.

"Thanks for showing me the problem, Joachim." The front door opened. "Right now, I need to check on my mother."

Sarah stepped back into the basement and pulled the door closed behind her.

Hovering on the top step, her heart nearly pounded out of her chest.

Footsteps sounded in the hallway. Was Victor heading up the stairs or coming into the kitchen?

Sarah clutched her stomach to still its rumblings.

He entered the kitchen. Glasses clinked. Water ran in the sink. She heard movement below and glanced down, seeing a small, brown creature with a long tail run across the floor. Sarah pretended rats didn't bother her when she was with Victor, but she didn't like rodents of any kind, especially ones with beady eyes and long tails. Her gaze landed on something else that troubled her—an old tin of rat poison sat open on a workbench. Victor must have used the poison to control the rats in the house.

She thought of Ms. Hazel's lethargy and rapid decline. The woman's shallow complexion was troubling, as well.

Was Victor poisoning the rats…and his mother?

Sarah gripped the basement handrail as a wave of vertigo swept over her. The rapid pounding of her heart and her accelerated pulse were probably making her feel woozy. The walls started to cave in around her in a sweep of claustrophobia.

She closed her eyes, hoping that might calm her anxiety, but it only made the symptoms worse. She gripped the handrail more tightly and opened her eyes to get her bearings.

Victor's footsteps came again. This time, he neared the basement door. She glanced down, seeing the doorknob turn.

*No!* she silently screamed.

The phone rang. A landline. Victor hurried into the front parlor to answer the phone.

Sarah had only a minute or two. Opening the door, she crossed the kitchen and slipped outside. She didn't look back to see if she could find Joachim. She had to get away, back to the path before Victor returned to the kitchen.

The memory of being held captive flashed through her mind. The attic room, the dark nights she lay hearing the rodents running through the attic. The candle Victor would bring to light the room, knowing she was terrified of the open flame.

She couldn't and wouldn't go back again. No matter what happened, she needed to remain free.

What about the scratching in the basement? Brushing it off as rats would make everything so much easier. But she had been held against her will. What if Victor were holding another person? A chill scurried down her spine. What if the sounds were a call for help from someone beyond the padlocked door? Sarah couldn't ignore her gut feelings nor the sounds. She had to find a way to learn where that door led. Maybe then she'd know if another woman was being held captive.

# NINE

The day could not pass fast enough for Joachim. He had watched Sarah run out of Victor's house and scurry back to the path. Just as she disappeared into the woods, Victor had stepped onto the porch, demanding to know why Joachim was not working.

He had welcomed the chastisement. It showed that Victor had no idea who had been in the house. Sarah had made it safely to the path and, hopefully, had made it home, as well.

A storm blew in later in the afternoon, which provided a good reason for Joachim to pack up his tools earlier than he would have normally. Victor had grumbled, but the dark billowing clouds and flashes of lightning that ripped across the sky overrode his discontent.

Belle was skittish on the way home as thunder clashed overhead. A car raced by much too fast, throwing water against the buggy. If only the *Englisch* realized how their cars could unsettle a horse, they might be a bit more cautious. Too many accidents happened on back roads even in good weather; add water to the mix and the situation got even more risky.

Joachim thought again of the fateful night his brother had died so tragically. Had the driver of the other vehicle been tried for recklessness? Probably not. The Amish with their slower moving buggies usually bore the blame, and the cases rarely went to court.

His spirits were bolstered when he turned onto his father's property. He leaped from the buggy and hurried to the back door, needing to assure himself that Sarah was there before he tended to his mare.

He pushed open the door.

She stood at the dry sink, kneading dough. His unexpected entrance startled her. A gasp escaped her lips, but when she turned and recognized him, her fear disappeared and was replaced with an awareness that connected them just as had happened that first time she had glanced at him from inside the Thomin home. Joachim's chest constricted, and the world stood still for one electrifying moment.

Sarah was on an emotional roller coaster. Hearing movement behind her, she feared Victor had entered the Burkholder kitchen. When she turned, her eyes locked on Joachim, standing there baring his soul in the intensity of his gaze. Her heart stopped beating for one brief second as if both of them were suspended in time and had gone someplace far away from the fear and confusion that had existed in her life for too long.

"Joachim, I thought you were someone else." She raised her hand and patted her chest as if to start her heart beating again. "You scared me."

He seemed to search for words, and then shook his head and headed back outside to his buggy. Had she said something wrong?

Hurrying to the window, she watched him lead his mare into the barn. Knowing Joachim, he would remain there caring for his horse while she wondered what had transpired. The moment of connection had taken her to a special place only to have his rejection topple her back to the reality of the moment. She was foolish to give her feelings such free rein. After her mother's less than wise choices in male companions, Sarah had shielded her heart. Now here in this Amish home, she had let down her guard and was making another huge mistake.

She turned from the window and picked up the dough only to slam it down on the dry sink and pound her fists into the plump flour mix. Over and over again, she pushed and folded and stretched the dough until her arms ached from the strain. Kneading the dough eased her frustration until the door opened again. This time she could sense Joachim's presence even without seeing him, as if there had been a trigger within her body signaling his nearness. How could she hide her true feelings if even her body gave her away?

She dropped the dough into a greased mixing bowl, covered it with a dish towel and placed it on the back of the stove, where the warmth could help the yeast to rise.

She turned and tried to smile in spite of the tangle of confusion that swirled within her.

"Let me wash my hands, and then we'll have coffee." She struggled to hide her inner turmoil. "Rebecca is gathering potatoes from the root cellar. Although she also planned to clean the shelves and rearrange the canned goods. She said the task would take quite some time. While she is gone, we need to talk. But first I must tell you what I heard while I was in Victor's basement."

*Talk?* Joachim wondered what Sarah wanted to discuss and what she had heard. He took a seat at the table and watched as she filled two mugs and placed one in front of him.

"You take yours black?" she asked.

He nodded and waited as she added cream from the

pitcher to her own cup and a teaspoon of sugar. After stirring the hot brew, she reached for a plate of cookies on the counter and placed both the plate and her cup on the table as she slid effortlessly into the chair across from him.

"I apologize for startling you earlier," he said. "I hurried inside to ensure you were home and all right. The last I saw, you were running toward the path. I stood by the door ready to distract Victor in case he came outside."

"He remained on the phone?"

"For only a minute or two, talking to someone named George."

Sarah's eye widened. "George is the man who is supposed to bring Miriam here. Did you hear him mention my sister's name?"

"I only heard a bit of the conversation and nothing about Miriam. Victor disconnected and stepped outside just as you disappeared into the woods. I feared he had seen you, but his only concern was my need to get back to work. Thankfully, the storm came up this afternoon so I could come home early."

She touched his sleeve. "You are wet from the rain."

"*Yah*, and from the cars that sped around the buggy, never realizing the water their tires stir up."

"Perhaps you should change into something dry."

He shook his head. "You said we should talk. What do you want to discuss?"

She leaned in closer. "What I heard in the basement."

"You heard Victor talking to me, no doubt."

"Only your muffled voices. I ran to the far end of the basement, needing to hide in case Victor came downstairs. I thought he might have heard the basement door close. Thankfully, the water ran in the sink. The sound must have drowned out the closing door."

"I was sure he would not believe that my only reason for

being inside was to draw water into a glass. As hateful as Victor seems, he can be a bit of a *dummkopf*, as we say."

Sarah wrinkled her brow. "I need a translation."

"Stupid. A dummy who lacks common sense. His father was a learned man, well-thought-of in the local community. His mother was known for her big heart and sweet disposition. Somehow Victor missed out on the fine qualities seen in both parents."

"Children do not always take after their parents, which is a relief to me," Sarah said. "I never wanted to be like my mother."

"She was an authoritarian and demanding of you?" he asked.

"Not really. I longed for structure and stability, but she could never settle down. We were nomads traveling from one rental property to another across the United States. Two or three months in one place was the norm. Then my mother would become dissatisfied and decide it was time to move. Often the bills she couldn't pay would mount up, and she'd wake us in the middle of the night so we could sneak out of town undetected."

"I left this area five years ago," he shared. "Before that, this house was the only home I had known."

Sarah smiled. "We're both so different."

"Yet sometimes opposites are attracted to one another."

She glanced down as if unsure of how to reply, perhaps even unsure what he was alluding to with the comment. Joachim understood her confusion. An Amish man and an *Englisch* woman were as extreme opposites as two people could be. They had found each other because of her need to escape and his willingness to come to her aid. Otherwise, it was unlikely their paths would ever have crossed.

"We have gotten off the topic," she quickly added. "I

wanted to tell you what I heard in the basement other than your mumbling voices."

He raised his cup to his lips and took a long pull while she gathered her thoughts.

"I have been in the basement before," Sarah began, "but Victor has always gone with me. Ms. Hazel kept extra canned goods there, so I would help Victor carry the items upstairs. One day we saw a rodent. He was especially unsettled by the small creature."

"This is what happened today. The mouse frightened him."

Sarah nodded. "His house is infested with rodents, so he has reason to be anxious. Ms. Hazel kept old rusted tins of rat poison in the basement. The kind that contains arsenic, although I'm not sure how effective it might be as old as the cans look. Today the poison sat open on a basement workbench."

"Which means he is trying to solve his rat problem."

"Probably. I went to the very back of the basement where I hadn't been before. That's when I heard the noise."

"A rat?"

"Maybe, but I don't think so. It was a scratching sound. I found a corner alcove and a doorway."

"You opened the door?"

"I couldn't. A metal bar ran from one side of the wall to the other and was padlocked. I looked but couldn't find a key."

"A secret room perhaps?"

"I'm not sure. Could it be a door that leads outside?"

Joachim shook his head. "I have been all around the house, checking for damage, and have not found a door from the basement level. The only entrances appear to be the one that leads to the kitchen and the other into the main foyer. Besides, the basement sits almost entirely belowground. Stairs would be needed, or a ramp to climb from the basement to ground level. I have seen nothing like that which you have mentioned."

"It's an old house, Joachim. Perhaps the stairway has been filled in."

"This could be, but then the door would lead nowhere. Are you sure the scratching sounds came from behind the door? The basement is large. A sound on one side could echo in another area. Besides, a scratching sound does not mean a human being is involved, especially when rats and other rodents seem to have taken up residence in the house."

She sighed. "It sounds crazy, doesn't it? You probably think I'm a *dummkopf*, like Victor."

Joachim laughed. "You could never be like Victor, nor do I think you are being foolish. Maybe you heard exactly what you think. Victor is an evil man, and it would not be surprising if there are other victims of his cruelty. But it is also possible that your fear is causing you to jump to conclusions. You were held captive for a period of time. Perhaps you heard a sound, but your imagination took it to the extreme. You have a big heart, Sarah, and would not want another human to be held against his or her will. I will check the outside of the house tomorrow and will look for anything that could have been filled in or a door that could have been walled off. If I see something, I will let you know."

He hesitated. "The Amish are not prone to calling in law enforcement, but so much has happened. I understand you want to avoid the police, but..."

"I can't and I won't trust the local law enforcement. Victor said the police were involved. They might tell Victor where to find me."

"Suppose Victor captures someone else?"

"Perhaps he already has, if the sound I heard in the basement was caused by another person."

"Then all the more reason to involve the police."

"Maybe when I'm ready to leave and return to Tennessee."

"You are not leaving any time soon?"

"I can't stay here much longer, Joachim. I need to find my sister Miriam, if she's even alive. I also have an older sister, Hannah, who left the family three years ago. She was going to Atlanta. I might find her there."

"Atlanta is a big city. A person could get lost in such a place."

"Are you saying I shouldn't try to find Hannah?"

"I would think involving law enforcement might be the best way to find both your sisters."

"Corrupt law enforcement won't help me, Joachim. I would have to trust the person I tell."

"You have told me, which must mean you trust me."

She smiled. "You saved me, Joachim. You could have revealed my whereabouts to Victor a number of times, and instead you've chosen to keep me safe. I have to trust you. At least for now."

She scooped up the empty mugs and took them to the sink just as Rebecca entered the house, carrying a basket filled with potatoes. Her face was flushed. Levi followed her inside. He was laughing as if he did not have a care in the world. Would Sarah ever be able to laugh with such abandonment, or would she carry the weight of all that had happened on her shoulders forever?

# TEN

"Is something wrong, Joachim?"

Rebecca stood staring at him. Her smile was gone, and she looked concerned as she glanced from him to Sarah. "Did something else happen? Did Victor come to the house again?"

He shook his head. "I left Victor at his mother's house."

"Yet you look as if something is very wrong."

He glanced at Sarah, giving her the opportunity to share what was troubling her.

"The coffee is hot," she said, as if to deflect the tension that filled the room.

Levi grabbed a cup from the cabinet and headed to the stove. Sarah filled his cup, refilled hers and Joachim's, and then poured coffee for Rebecca.

His sister seemed surprised to be the one served for a change. "You should sit at the table, Sarah, and let me pour the coffee," Rebecca said. "I am not used to being waited on."

Sarah smiled and appeared to appreciate Rebecca's comment. "You and Joachim have done so much for me. It is the least I can do."

When everyone was at the table, sipping coffee, Sarah joined them and waited for a lull in the conversation before asking, "Do you remember seeing a basement door at the Thomin house?"

She looked at Levi. "Did your sister ever mention the basement?"

He shook his head. "I cannot remember Naomi saying anything about the basement. Why do you ask?"

"Joachim and I wanted to ensure Victor's mother was all right. Victor was away, so we went to check on her. We found her empty prescription bottles that Victor has not refilled. We also found sleeping pills. As lethargic as his mother has been, I fear he might be sedating her."

Rebecca sighed and shook her head. "Victor is not to be trusted, that is for certain. It troubles me deeply that he might not be providing adequate care for his mother."

"It troubles me, as well. But there is something else." Sarah recounted hiding in the basement and the scratching sounds she heard.

"Surely it was the rats that you say have nested in the house," Levi suggested. "Perhaps Victor needs a few cats to scare the rodents away."

"It sounds as if more than one cat would be needed," Rebecca added.

Sarah nodded and then continued, "The barricaded door could lead to a storage closet, but it could, at one time, have been an outside exit from the cellar. Do either of you recall hearing of a basement door on the exterior of the house in years past?"

Levi shook his head. "I have not seen a basement exit, although I do not recall ever walking around the house. A few times, I took the buggy and picked up Naomi after she finished working. She always came out of the kitchen door."

Rebecca nodded in agreement. "I have been to the kitchen entrance, but have not walked around the house either. Nor would I have had any need to look for an old door. But I do know someone who might provide information."

Joachim leaned closer. "Someone in the area?"

"*Yah*, that is so. Do you remember Mamie Carver, the *Englisch* woman who used to buy eggs from me?"

"The Carver family lived in a small house that sat back from the road. As I recall, they rented a tract of land from the Koenigs and grew vegetables that Mamie's mother canned."

Rebecca nodded. "That is right. Her mother died a few years ago, and Mamie's eyesight is failing, but she is still able to tend her garden. You must visit her, Joachim."

"How would she be able to help us?" Sarah asked.

"Her mother worked for Ms. Hazel's parents, who owned the home before Ms. Hazel married. Miss Carver's grandmother worked there, as well."

Sarah's face brightened. "So she might recall information about the basement."

"Perhaps she visited the house. It was customary for the owners of the big houses to provide for their staffs at Christmastime. Often there would be a day of celebration with food and activities. The children of those employed on the property would take part. Miss Carver may have been involved, or she might recall her mother or grandmother talking about the event."

Sarah glanced at Joachim. "We must find Mamie and talk to her."

"Tomorrow. If the rain continues, Victor will not expect me to work."

"And if the sun shines?" Sarah asked.

"I will work in the morning and tell him I must tend to my father's farm in the afternoon."

He glanced at Levi. "You will be here?"

"*Yah*, I told your *datt* that I would help Rebecca with the chores until he returns with your *mamm*. He knows that day after tomorrow I must go to Willkommen to help my uncle at the Amish Market."

Joachim's heart sunk. "Day after tomorrow? Our *datt* is returning home that soon?"

"This I do not know for sure," Levi admitted. "I only told him when I would be gone."

"You know our parents," Rebecca added. "They only schedule when they will go on their visits. They rarely plan their return."

Joachim nodded. What his sister had said was true. His parents could stay away longer…but perhaps not. Which meant it might be no more than forty-eight hours until Joachim would have to talk to his father. If their meeting did not go well, Joachim might be forced to leave home again. He glanced at Sarah, knowing he was not ready to leave her.

He would hold on to each precious hour. There was so little time. Would it be enough time to tell Sarah how he felt? Or would he leave never sharing how special she was to him?

# ELEVEN

The deep rumble of thunder woke Sarah before the first light of dawn. Rain fell in torrents, but she was grateful for the downpour. The storm would provide a reason Joachim would not be able to work for Victor today.

She and Joachim needed to visit Miss Carver and learn more about the padlocked doorway. Sarah thought again about yesterday when she heard the scratching noise. Could the sound have been made by a mouse or a rat or some other creature?

Throwing back the quilt and sheet, she dropped her feet to the floor and reached for the flashlight, grateful again for Joachim's thoughtfulness. She hadn't wanted to tell him about her childhood and the fear that still troubled her.

The fact that her mother had never again mentioned the incident had made it even more difficult to bear. She longed to be forgiven, but forgiveness had never been provided.

Once she had mustered the courage to mention the fire to Miriam. Even her sister had shoved aside her comment. "That was the past," Miriam had told Sarah. "We need to focus on the present."

But the guilt she carried had followed Sarah into the present and remained a weight around her neck. No matter how hard she tried, Sarah would never be rid of the memory.

Footsteps sounded in the hallway. From the lightness of the step, Rebecca was hurrying downstairs to add wood to the stove and begin her day of cooking. Sarah dressed quickly and followed her to the kitchen.

The tin coffeepot sat on the burner. Water dripped through the grounds and filled the house with the rich scent of the morning brew.

"You are up early," Rebecca said in greeting. Her eyes were bright and her smile welcoming. Levi had stayed after dinner last night, and the two of them had sat on the front porch until well after sundown. Sarah envied the relationship they had, an easy and familiar connection even when they weren't conversing. A bond connected them as surely as if their hearts were actually tied together with a ribbon.

As much as Sarah longed to have someone in her life to lean on, she couldn't trust her instincts. She had seen the destruction caused by love wrongly given. That was one of the reasons she had encouraged her mother and Miriam to drive to Willkommen. Sarah had wanted to find her long-lost aunt, her mother's sister, but she had also wanted to breathe new life into her own daily routine. Secretly, she had dreamed of remaining with her aunt when her mother and Miriam returned home. Foolish though it seemed, she had hoped the rural mountain community would provide an opportunity for her to start fresh without the constant shadow of her mother's disapproval.

She poured coffee into a mug and sighed as she reached for the pitcher and added a dollop of the rich cream and a teaspoon of sugar.

Now she wondered if she would have stayed in Willkommen if Miriam and her mother returned home to Tennessee. Sarah had relied on Miriam to guide her through the first twenty-one years of her life. It was doubtful to think Sarah would have become more independent in Willkommen.

"You seem pensive this morning." Rebecca's statement pulled her from her thoughts.

"I'm still tired," Sarah admitted.

"You should have slept longer."

"I wanted to help you with breakfast, yet here I am pining over my coffee. What can I do?"

"We have bread from yesterday. Joachim likes it with butter and jelly. Could you fetch the butter from outside? It sits in a jar in the cool tub of water near the pump. You'll find a bottle of milk there, too. Bring both inside, if you do not mind."

Sarah glanced out the window. The pitter-patter of rain on the tin roof of the kitchen had eased, although the sky remained gray and overcast. She opened the door and stepped into the damp morning air, relishing the clear freshness of a new day washed clean by the earlier storm.

She hurried down the steps and followed the well-worn path to the pump. To the side was a tin tub half filled with cold water, as Rebecca had mentioned. The butter sat in a half-submerged glass jar next to the milk jug. She lifted both from the tub, shook off the excess moisture and turned back to the house.

The sound of a car's engine made her heart lurch. She hurried for the protection of the porch and ducked behind the railing, her eyes straining to see the vehicle on the road this early. Surely it wasn't a red pickup.

Peering through the gaps between the fence posts, she realized her folly. If Victor was on the road and turned his truck into the Burkholder farm, she would be seen instantly.

She held her breath and stared at the road as the sound of the engine grew louder.

"Please," she whispered.

A black sedan zipped along the roadway and passed the farm.

She let out the air she was holding and clutched the two jars close to her heart.

"Sarah?"

She jumped, nearly dropping the milk and butter. Hands reached to grab them and locked around her arms. When she looked up, she stared into Joachim's questioning eyes.

"I have startled you again," he said, contrition evident in his tone.

She tried to cover her surprise. "I thought you were still asleep."

"The Amish rise early. Animals must be fed and watered. Stalls mucked."

"You haven't forgotten about visiting Mamie Carver, have you?"

He smiled. "I have not forgotten. It appears more storms are brewing in the distant sky, which provide the excuse I need for Victor. He will not expect me this morning. After breakfast I will take the buggy to Miss Carver's home."

"I'll go with you," Sarah insisted.

"Storms may continue throughout the entire morning. You should remain here and stay dry."

"I'm not made of sugar, Joachim."

He laughed and his eyes glanced down at her shoes, wet from the rain. "You have not melted yet, that is true. You can go with me, but we must be careful in case Victor is on the road."

"He sleeps late and doesn't like to get his truck dirty when the roads are wet. I don't think we'll run into him."

"You know him well."

Sarah hesitated. Joachim was right. After weeks of being held captive, she knew Victor's idiosyncrasies, of which he had many. Somehow all that knowledge hadn't helped her escape until Joachim came into her life. She owed him her gratitude.

"I don't know if I ever thanked you for saving me. If you hadn't come along—"

"As I recall, Sarah, you were the one who snuck from the house and hid in the buggy. You saved yourself. The only thing I did was drive my buggy off Victor's property."

"Did you know I was hiding there?"

A smile twitched his lips. "I saw that the tarp had been moved. You had raised your finger to your lips when I glanced through the window. It was easy to realize you did not belong with Victor."

"He had grown increasingly antagonistic," she shared. "That particular morning, we were in the attic. I mentioned the rats, which probably added to his agitation. He choked me until I could not catch my breath. I knew then that I had to escape."

"Then I arrived at the perfect time."

She nodded, feeling the pull between them that made her want to step closer. Instead, the clip-clop of horses' hooves on the road caused her to draw back. She was too visible, especially with the sun rising in the east. She would be safer inside. And her heart would be safer if she put some distance between herself and Joachim. But was safety what she really wanted when it came to him? He had saved her. Was she letting down her guard because of what he had done? She would forever be grateful, but she could not confuse gratitude with affection.

"Rebecca is fixing breakfast," she said. "You must eat, then we will find Miss Carver and learn what we can about the Thomin basement."

"You still believe a person made the scratching sound?"

"I don't know, but I won't have peace until I ensure that no one else is being held captive."

She hurried up the stairs to the porch, relieved to have Joachim follow close behind her. For a moment, she thought of Rebecca and Levi entering the kitchen last night with that special bond between them so evident.

Would Rebecca be aware of a connection between Joachim and Sarah? She sighed at her foolishness. She was putting too much emphasis on a moment in the early morning before she had a chance to think clearly. Joachim was Amish. His faith intrigued her, and if truth be known, he intrigued her as well, but the handsome carpenter needed to look for someone within his own community to capture his heart.

Sarah stamped her feet on the rug as she entered the sweet-smelling kitchen. She was acting like a *dummkopf.* Better to guard her heart and her head until she could get safely away—from Victor and perhaps from the handsome handyman, as well.

In a moment of weakness, Joachim had agreed to Sarah accompanying him to visit Miss Carver. Hopefully, he had not allowed his heart to override his head. Even if Victor usually slept late and kept his truck off the road during wet weather, the man's actions had become more erratic according to Sarah.

Joachim would never forgive himself if his moment of weakness, giving in to her pleading to come with him, put Sarah at risk. He blamed it on her crystal-blue eyes, which shimmered like a placid lake, reflecting the sun's bright rays. One glance at her and he was lost in another world, a world without the restrictions that came from an Amish man having interest in an *Englisch* woman. As much as Joachim needed to be Amish, he longed to be with Sarah.

Their time together was passing much too quickly. His father would be home soon. Joachim had moments of despondence when he was convinced he had been a fool to think reconciliation could be achieved. At other times he had hope that his father would accept him back. Pride was the wall that stood between them. At the present moment, Joachim believed his *datt* would not change his mind or his heart.

He sighed, pondering whether he had been foolish in coming home. Yet if he had not, he never would have met Sarah. The thought that she would still have been under Victor's control made Joachim grateful that he had journeyed back to his Amish roots. He only wished Sarah could embrace that which gave meaning to his own life. But a *fancy* woman could never embrace the *plain* life. Of this, he was sure.

# TWELVE

"I do not think this is a good idea," Rebecca told Sarah. Both women stood at the sink filled with breakfast dishes and peered through the kitchen window as Joachim disappeared into the barn to hitch Belle to the buggy.

"The sky is dark," Rebecca cautioned. "More rain will fall, and there will be lightning and thunder. Belle spooks in storms. You are tired and still healing from what you have endured. The seat of the buggy is not what you are used to. Stay here and let Joachim go alone to talk to Miss Carver."

Sarah appreciated Rebecca's concern, but she would not be content to stand at the window and watch for Joachim's return.

"Didn't you tell me that Miss Carver lives close?" Sarah asked. "Surely a short trip won't be a problem. Joachim was worried about me getting wet. You are concerned that I will not be comfortable in the buggy."

Her frustration mounted the more she thought about Rebecca's and Joachim's desires to coddle her.

"I was not comfortable locked in an attic room or being tied up in the passenger seat of Victor's truck," she said. "The drugs didn't help my comfort either, especially when I didn't have any food and reacted to the heavy medication on an empty stomach."

She hadn't intended to be so adamant, but she wasn't a prima donna. She had endured a lot over the last few weeks and none of it good.

Rebecca turned, her gaze filled with compassion. "I was thinking only of your well-being, Sarah, but you are right. You have endured so much. I am not sure I would have survived. You are a strong woman and independent. I was wrong to want to hold you back."

*Independent?*

No one had called her that before. "But I'm not strong," she countered. "I've always relied on my sister Miriam."

"Your sister was not with you at the Thomin house, *yah*? You escaped by yourself."

"I escaped because of Joachim."

Rebecca tilted her head. "You worked together to escape Victor. I want you to remain safe so that you and Joachim can share more moments in the future."

Sarah took a step back. "I can't think of the future, Rebecca. I can only think of today. Plus, I have to focus on the sound I heard. Suppose a person is being held captive? That's what's most important, not whether I am comfortable or dry."

"*Yah*, you are right. I will pray Victor is holding no other women against their will, and I will pray he does not find you again."

Rebecca grabbed the cape hanging on one of the pegs by the door and draped it over Sarah's shoulders. Reaching for the black bonnet, she smiled. "The wide bill will offer protection from buffeting winds. It will also keep you hidden from view should Victor be on the road." After tying the bonnet securely under Sarah's chin, Rebecca nodded her approval.

"It limits my vision." Sarah adjusted the bonnet, still mildly upset by Rebecca's somewhat overly protective nature. Then she felt embarrassed by her curt tone. Rebecca was merely concerned for her safety.

"I'm sorry, Rebecca. You're kind to let me wear your cape and bonnet. I'll get used to the wide bill, even if it limits my vision."

Rebecca chuckled. "A woman can sometimes hide her feelings within the hat."

"I doubt you want to hide your feelings from Levi." Sarah couldn't help but counter.

Rebecca's cheeks turned pink. "Levi is a good friend and a good man, but he has many women who are interested in him."

Sarah raised her brow. "Yet he comes here every day."

"Coming here is a job. My *datt* hired him."

"Your father did not tell him to have a twinkle in his eye or laughter on his lips. I've seen the way he looks at you."

"Do you mean he is laughing at me?" Rebecca's own eyes sparked with mischief.

"You know exactly what I mean."

"I see something in Joachim's gaze as well, when he looks at you. He has been away for five years, yet I know my *bruder*."

Sarah held up her hand. "Your *bruder*, as you say, came home to talk to your father. Anything you see in his gaze is his concern about how that meeting will turn out."

Rebecca lowered her eyes. "I worry about that meeting, as well. My *datt* is a strong man who has been deeply hurt by the death of his younger son." She glanced up. "He has also been hurt by the absence of his oldest son."

"Have you told Joachim?"

"Some things he must find out on his own. Besides, I see through my own eyes. Perhaps I do not see as Joachim would."

The sound of the buggy caused both women to glance

outside. "It is time to go." Sarah pulled the cape tight across her neck.

"I almost forgot." Rebecca ran to the pantry and returned with a basket draped with a dark blue cloth. "This is for Miss Carver. There is bread and cheese, eggs, butter, and a pie. She does not have anyone to help her with her baking."

"She'll enjoy the food, I'm sure. I'll tell Mamie you were thinking of her."

"Perhaps she can come for supper after my parents return. They would like to see her."

"Be careful while we are gone, Rebecca. I worry about your safety with Victor so close."

"I will lock the door. Do not worry about me. Take care yourself." She readjusted the bonnet around Sarah's face.

Her thoughtfulness touched Sarah. Without forethought, she hugged Rebecca. "Be on guard lest Victor comes searching for me. You must remain safe."

"*Gott* will provide," Rebecca said as the two women parted.

Sarah opened the kitchen door and stepped onto the porch, thinking of Rebecca's words. God hadn't provided protection for her mother or Miriam or herself when they had been carjacked. Would He protect Rebecca today? What about Joachim?

All of them were in danger, and it was because of Sarah. She had brought danger to this peaceful Amish farm. She had been thinking only about herself and her own well-being. She hadn't truly considered Rebecca's or Joachim's safety.

The last thing she wanted was to have anything harmful happen to either of them. Rebecca was a lovely woman who had a full life ahead of her with Levi, even if she wasn't ready to admit that. And Joachim?

He had so much to offer a woman. The right woman. An Amish woman to whom he could give his heart.

If only Sarah could be part of his future, but that was a silly thought that needed to be erased from her mind.

Joachim helped Sarah into the buggy and climbed in next to her. He spread a protective throw over her legs.

"The rain won't hurt me, Joachim," she politely informed him.

"*Yah*, but you have not ridden in the front of an Amish buggy when so much moisture covers the road. The cars do not understand how their wheels throw the water. I do not want you drowning before we talk to Miss Carver."

She laughed. Not what he had expected.

"You think my words are funny?" he asked.

She shook her head and touched his arm. He liked the feel of her fingers and the way she leaned into him. Perhaps riding together was a good idea after all.

"I wasn't making fun, Joachim. I was laughing about the seriousness of your expression. You are always so concerned about my safety."

He relaxed a bit and allowed his mouth to turn up in a responsive smile. "I have never found anyone else in the back of my buggy, Sarah Miller. There is a certain amount of responsibility I must take to ensure you remain safe and protected. Do you consider this a bad thing or an inconvenience?"

Her fingers rubbed his arm, making a ripple of current flow along his spine. She had too much of an effect on him, especially sitting so close.

"I've never had anyone concerned about me before, Joachim." Suddenly, her face was serious, and her words struck an even deeper chord within him. He stared into her eyes and lost all sense of time and space and where they were to go and why they were going there. Instead, all he could focus on was her beauty and the pureness of her gaze and the way his heart lurched whenever she smiled.

Rebecca opened the kitchen door and pulled him back to reality. "Sarah, you forgot the basket."

She seemed equally as confused as she pulled her eyes away from Joachim and glanced at Rebecca. "Oh yes, I'm sorry. I wasn't thinking."

Joachim hoped she *had* been thinking, thinking about him.

He took the basket from his sister's outstretched hand and placed it on the floor of the buggy behind them. After waving farewell to Rebecca, he reached for the reins and with a flick of his wrist, Belle trotted along the drive. He pulled her up a bit at the edge of the road to check traffic in both directions before the buggy turned onto the main road.

"We will hope the rain will keep the *Englischers* with their big cars at home," Joachim said, steering the conversation to practical matters of the head instead of the heart.

"Rebecca said Miss Carver's house is not far."

"Not far in miles, but the drive will take time. You are used to vehicles with engines. We have only Belle."

"She'll get us there," Sarah said with confidence.

Joachim liked her optimism. He smiled again and flicked the reins. Belle increased her speed to a steady trot and ambled along the roadway, heading away from Petersville and the Thomin home toward the cluster of Amish farms. Would Sarah appreciate the beauty of the land and the bounty of *Gott*'s providence for providing such a fertile area to farm?

Joachim hoped she would. He wanted her to like everything about the Amish and their way of life. The truth was he wanted her to like him, as well.

# THIRTEEN

The Amish farms rolled by one after another, each picturesque in its simplicity. Young children stood on their front porches and watched, wide-eyed as the buggy passed.

Sarah inhaled the country air and the musky smell of the red Georgia clay. Joachim seemed lost in thought, so she kept her gaze on the homes they passed. She wondered about the women working in the kitchens or helping the farmers in the field. Had they been raised Amish or had some of them lived the life she knew? If so, how had they decided to embrace the *plain* life? Surely the transition would be a challenge, yet she had found nothing difficult about being in the Burkholder home. She would have liked a mirror to check that her bonnet was on straight, but she could see enough of her reflection in the windowpane. She had never worn makeup or done much with her hair, so that wasn't a problem.

Sometimes she caught Joachim looking at her, and his gaze made her realize she must have done something right concerning her grooming, even without a mirror.

"The farms are lovely, Joachim. You will have one someday like your father?"

"*Yah*, although I like working with wood so I would have fewer fields and a larger workshop for my carpentry."

"You did carpentry work while you were away?"

"I did. There was more than enough work."

"Do you plan to stay here in the Petersville area or return to the Carolinas?"

"It depends upon my father. If he will have me in his house again, then I will stay."

"And if not?" she asked.

"Then I will find my own way and a new place to live."

"But you will remain Amish?"

"*Yah*, Amish is who I am."

For some reason, his response took the joy she had been feeling out of her heart.

Joachim turned the buggy onto a dirt side road and encouraged Belle onward. The path was pockmarked, and the ride became bumpy. Sarah bounced from side to side and began to understand Rebecca's concern about the buggy ride.

When the back wheel dropped into an especially large hole, she gasped and reached for the handle on the seat to steady herself.

"Do people ever fall off?" she asked in all seriousness.

Joachim put his arm around her and drew her closer. "I will not let you fall."

His words and the strength of his touch relieved her concern. She settled against him. In spite of the bumpy road, she liked sitting close to Joachim.

The ride soon came to an end at a small house. A tin roof hug over the raised porch and cast the door and two windows in shadow. A wooden rocking chair sat idle as Joachim helped Sarah climb from the buggy.

"The house could use some repair." Joachim kept his voice low. "I will come back with my tools once I have finished at the Thomin home."

He rapped on the door. "Miss Carver, it is Joachim

Burkholder and a friend. We have brought food from my sister, Rebecca."

Silence greeted them. Joachim knocked again. He glanced at Sarah and then over his shoulder, eyeing the road they had just traveled. "I will check the barn. You stay here."

"I'll go with you."

He nodded, but before they left the porch, the sound of footsteps caused them to glance at the corner of the house. A wizened woman appeared, stooped with age; her white hair contrasted sharply with her brown skin. She carried firewood and seemed out of breath with the effort. Seeing that she had company, her eyes widened and a smile pulled across her full face.

"Don't know if my eyes are making a fool of me, but I see Joachim Burkholder standing on my front porch big as life."

Sarah smiled at the humor in the woman's tone.

"Your eyes have not fooled you," Joachim responded as he flashed an equally warm smile back at the sweet woman. "I have come home."

Mamie nodded. Her gaze fell to Sarah. "And you have brought a pretty girlfriend to brighten my day."

Joachim hurried to where Mamie stood and took the wood from her hands. "You have a heavy load. Allow me the pleasure of helping you."

Mamie laughed. "You can help me any time, Joachim. Any time at all."

She climbed the stairs and held out her hand to Sarah. "Mamie Carver, ma'am."

"My name is Sarah," she replied, feeling strength in the woman's handshake and seeing the twinkle in her eyes. Miss Carver might be advanced in years, but she still had a spring in her step and a charisma that made Sarah feel instantly at home.

"Come inside. The coffee is hot. Joachim, you can set that firewood by the stove. Don't mind Butch. He's old, but friendly."

Sarah bent to pet the beagle who ambled toward them after Mamie opened the door.

"You would like Angelo," Sarah told the pup. "He's small, but friendly."

"Butch used to be a good hunter," Mamie bragged. "Now his nose doesn't smell much. Same as mine. Although I'd be interested to know what's in that basket you're carrying."

Sarah laughed. "Rebecca's pie and fresh baked bread, cheese and butter. Also some eggs."

"Which I appreciate. You folks come in and sit a spell."

She motioned them into the small but tidy house. The kitchen was to the left. A table and four chairs sat in the middle of the room with a stone fireplace to the right. Close to the hearth was a second rocking chair with a straight-back chair positioned nearby.

Peering through an open door, Sarah noticed a small bedroom. The single bed was covered with a quilt, and a latched rug covered the floor.

Sarah slipped out of her cape and took off her bonnet.

"Sit at the table, please." Mamie pointed her toward a chair. "I'll pour coffee."

"May I help?" Sarah asked.

"I'd like that. Milk's in the refrigerator. There's sugar on the counter. Why don't you slice that bread Rebecca made? I haven't had breakfast, and I'm hungry. Surely you and Joachim would like something to eat, as well."

"I'm still full from breakfast," Sarah and Joachim said in unison and then laughed.

Sarah opened a cabinet and found a plate and a serrated knife in the drawer next to the sink. She cut a thick slice of bread and slathered it with butter and strawberry preserves Rebecca had thoughtfully included.

As Mamie poured three cups of coffee, Sarah peered into the pantry and noticed the near-empty shelves, making a mental note to share the information with Rebecca.

Once Mamie finished eating her bread, she took a long drink from her coffee and wiped her hand over her mouth.

"Joachim, your sister makes pies like my mama and grandmamma used to make. Mama always said it was the lard that made her crust so flakey. Now the doctors tell us lard is bad for our health."

"Do you have any brothers or sisters?" Sarah inquired.

"I've got a younger brother. He and his wife live near Willkommen. I don't see much of them these days. His wife has rheumatism and stays close to home."

Sarah perked up at the mention of Willkommen. "Do you know of anyone named Annie Miller in that town?"

"Not that I recall, although I don't know many folks on that side of the mountains. Next time I see my brother, I could ask him. Is she a friend of yours?"

"My mother's sister."

"Yet you don't know her, child?"

"My mother left home at a young age. She never returned to this area. In fact, she never told us that she even had a sister until not long ago."

"Sometimes we stay away for a number of reasons." Mamie glanced knowingly at Joachim.

"And sometimes we return home seeking to mend any broken fences," Joachim added.

"Which is a very good thing," Mamie stated with a nod. "The good Lord says not to focus on the speck in another's eye, but rather to recognize the plank in our own. My brother and I had a tiff some years back. Can't remember what it was about. One day, I drove to his house. Even before he could say hello, I told him I was sorry. I wanted the divide between us to end."

"What happened?" Sarah leaned closer. She noticed Joachim was focused on the old woman's story, as well.

"My brother just stood there looking at me. In fact, he paused so long I was ready to turn around and get back in my car. Before I did, he stepped toward me, looked deep into my eyes and said he was sorry for the time we had wasted with the anger. He said it was time for healing. Then he pulled me into a bear hug, and we both laughed until tears ran from our eyes."

She stared at Joachim for a long moment, then turned her gaze to Sarah. "Your mama would do well to reconnect with her family."

Sadness flitted over Sarah. "She was killed not long ago."

"Oh, child, I'm so sorry. I saw pain in your eyes. I didn't know the reason. You need to find your aunt and be that conduit of peace and unity in the family. You can bridge the gap even after all those years."

"But suppose I can't find her?"

"Have you asked the Lord's help? He listens and responds when the request is for our good. I'll ask Him to help you."

Warmth swept over Sarah. A feeling of being loved, which was something she always had hoped to feel from her own mother. Miriam and Hannah had loved her but not in the same way as a parent, and she'd always felt the lack. Mamie, a sweet woman who had only just come into Sarah's life, had shown her how to fill the hole in her heart. Sarah needed to put her trust in the Lord.

Mamie covered Sarah's hand with her own and squeezed

ever so gently. "You turn to God with your needs, child. He'll make everything right. I know what I'm talking about."

She glanced at Joachim. "Your father made a mistake. You reacted because you were young and hurt by Eli's death and your own confusion. I'm glad you've come home."

"*Yah*, but my *datt* is visiting relatives. He and my *mamm* return home in a day or two. I am not sure how he will react to seeing me again."

"In his heart, he loves you. Remember that, Joachim. You are his son."

"But you know my father is a proud man."

"What does scripture tell us? *Pride goeth before a fall.*" She nodded as if appreciating her own wisdom. "You ask the Lord to make you the better man, Joachim. You can do that. But first, you must erase any pride in your own heart."

As Mamie took another drink from her cup, Sarah scooted closer. "There is something else we need to ask you, Miss Carver. Rebecca and Joachim told me that your grandmother and mother worked for Ms. Hazel Thomin's parents. Perhaps you went to the house as a girl?"

She nodded. "Sometimes I helped to move furniture or polish shoes or the silver. A house that big takes constant care. After Mr. Thomin passed, Ms. Hazel needed even more help. My brother and I were there often." She rubbed her cheek. "If you see Ms. Hazel, you tell her I said hello. She's a good woman."

"Her health has declined and she's bedridden," Sarah said.

"I'm so sorry about her failing health. I heard Naomi Plank was caring for her."

"Naomi left the area almost a year ago."

"Then who's taking care of Ms. Hazel?" Mamie narrowed her gaze. "Don't tell me that son of hers is back."

"That's the problem," Sarah said. "He *is* back, and I worry that he's not giving her good enough care."

"I'd like to give him a piece of my mind."

Sarah smiled, knowing Mamie would not mince words with Victor about his lack of concern for his mother. "We need your help on something else, Mamie, that involves Ms. Hazel's home."

Joachim leaned closer. "I am making repairs to the Thomin house. There is a boarded-up doorway in the basement, but I cannot see an opening on the outside of the structure. Do you recall a door leading from the basement?"

Mamie shook her head. "The only doors to the outside that I knew about were the one leading into the main hallway and the kitchen door. I've been in the basement enough to know I had to leave the house by the back door."

"Was there a closet or cubbyhole, perhaps?" Sarah asked.

"I wish I could help you, but nothing comes to mind."

Discouraged, Sarah glanced at Joachim. He nodded as if it was time for them to head back to the farm.

"Is there anything we can do for you before we leave?" Sarah asked, grabbing her mug and Joachim's off the table.

"You can pour me another cup of coffee and bring me my Bible." Mamie pointed to a small table near the rocker by the fireplace. "And my glasses. I always take time to read the Lord's word each day. My eyes may be bad, but not so bad that I can't read my scripture. The Lord always has something to tell me."

"I wish He would tell us about the basement," Sarah admitted as she quickly washed the mugs at the sink and placed them in the strainer. After drying her hands, she poured Miss Carver a fresh cup of coffee and placed it on the table, along with the Bible and glasses.

"Don't forget to take that basket back to Rebecca," Mamie added. "Hopefully, she will take pity on an old woman and bring me another pie in a week or so." Her eyes twinkled.

"I'll be sure to let Rebecca know how much you enjoyed what she provided. I'll also tell her that her pie rivaled your mother's. I'm sure Ms. Hazel loved your mother's pies, too."

Mamie chuckled. "You've got that right. Ms. Hazel would come to the kitchen house in the summer just to check on when the pies would be pulled from the oven. Course I'd be waiting on them, too."

"The kitchen house?" Sarah asked.

Mamie nodded. "It sat about thirty yards from the big house. Stoves gave off too much heat in summer before air-conditioning to be attached to the main house. The old homes all had a free-standing kitchen used in the summer. The root cellar was there. My mama used to send me down to get the apples for the pies. Mighty nice to have an excuse to visit a cool spot in the heat of the summer."

"Where exactly was the kitchen house located?" Joachim pressed.

Mamie thought for a moment. "To the rear of the house, but more to the east side so the hot afternoon sun wouldn't shine on it. The cool of the shade trees would help, too."

Joachim glanced at Sarah. She shook her head. "I'm not good at understanding distances, but it seems that was a long way to carry food back to the house. What happened if it rained?"

"Why, they used the tunnel when it rained," Mamie was quick to reply.

Sarah looked at Joachim. "A tunnel? From the root cellar?"

Mamie nodded. “Sure enough. It led to the big house so when the rain came, the food could be carried to the dining room without getting wet.”

“But the tunnel didn’t lead to the dining room,” Sarah said.

“No.” Mamie shook her head. “The tunnel led to the basement.”

# FOURTEEN

After saying goodbye to Mamie Carver, Joachim helped Sarah into the buggy and guided Belle along the dirt path to the main road. More rain had fallen while they were inside, and a thin layer of water lay across the asphalt once they turned onto the main road.

"The barricaded door has to lead to the tunnel," Sarah said as she adjusted the bonnet on her head and pulled the cape tight around her neck. "But I never noticed a kitchen house."

"Mamie talked about it sitting in the shade under trees. Perhaps the woods have grown around the old structure. Or maybe it was torn down when air-conditioning was installed and they did not need it anymore. The only buildings I know of are the barn and the few outbuildings located on that side of the house. Mr. Thomin was an expert carpenter. There is a wood shed nearby and also another small building that houses garden tools."

"Look around the grounds the next time you're there."

He nodded. "*Yah*, that I will do for certain."

The rain started again and the wind gusted, sending a sheet of water against the buggy. Sarah lowered her head against the pummeling rain.

Thunder rumbled overhead. Joachim hurried Belle. He needed to get Sarah home and out of the storm.

In the distance, the sound of an approaching car made his pulse quicken. *Please,* Gott.

Sarah lifted her gaze. Her face was lined with worry. "Surely it can't be Victor."

"It is probably someone else on the road, but no matter who it is, lower your head as the car passes," Joachim cautioned.

He flicked the reins to encourage Belle. The buggy creaked as the horse trotted up the small hill.

The approaching car crested the rise, taking up more than half of its lane. Joachim steered Belle to the edge of the road as the car zoomed past. It was a big, boxy SUV painted white, with tinted windows that made it impossible to see the driver or passengers.

The car was going much too fast for the narrow road. The wheels splashed a wave of water against the buggy, soaking both of them.

The SUV screeched to a stop. Joachim glanced back. Had the driver realized his mistake and stopped to offer an apology?

The SUV backed up and pulled next to the buggy. The driver's window rolled down partially, and a man peered through the opening. He had a full face and small eyes, which glared at Joachim from under bushy brows. A scar ran along his cheek and disappeared under his jaw.

From the frustration written so plainly across his face, rather than the remorse Joachim had hoped to see, the guy was probably not going to ask forgiveness for his negligent driving. Someone huddled in the back seat. Joachim could not see the person's features through the tinted glass, although the person did appear to have long hair.

"You folks know of a man name Victor Thomin?" the bushy browed guy asked. "I thought he lived along this road, but I can't find the turnoff to his house."

Sarah bristled at the mention of Victor's name.

"You must turn your vehicle around and head back toward Petersville, the way you came," Joachim replied. "You will see a brick mailbox on the left about two miles ahead. Turn onto that driveway. His house sits back from the main road."

The guy nodded but failed to offer thanks. Instead, he pulled his car into a nearby drive, backed onto the road and then gunned his engine and squealed past Joachim and Sarah, sending more water to splash over them. The close proximity of the massive car as it barreled past made Belle skittish. She pranced and shook her head, causing the buggy to edge off the road. The back wheel angled up a small rise.

The whole carriage tilted. Sarah screamed.

Joachim reached for her. Before he could grab her arm, she slipped through his hands and flew out of the buggy.

"Sarah." His heart lurched. He leaped to the pavement and knelt next to where she lay. Her eyes were closed, her mouth open ever so slightly.

"Sarah, are you all right?"

She moaned. Her eyelids fluttered open.

Relief swept over him. He touched her hand. "Tell me you can raise your hand."

She wrinkled her brow. "My hand…why?"

"Just do as I ask."

She raised one hand and then the other.

"What about your neck? Does anything hurt?"

"Everything hurts, but I didn't break anything—at least I don't think I did." She rolled to her side and started to raise herself.

"Go slowly. You had a bad fall." Joachim grabbed her arm and helped her stand.

She wobbled for a second and then brushed the dirt from her dress. “Rebecca’s pretty outfit is ruined.”

“It will wash. Are you sure you are all right?”

“Yes, but I’m getting cold. Who was that man?”

“One of Victor’s friends perhaps. You have seen him before?”

She shook her head. “Never. Did you notice someone in the back seat with long hair? I couldn’t see clearly through the windows. Do you think it was Miriam?”

“I do not know, but we must get you home now.”

Joachim lifted her into the buggy, overwhelmed with gratitude that Sarah had not been badly injured. Much as he did not want to think of another buggy accident, he could not help but remember what had happened five years earlier. Eli had lain on the road in almost the same way Sarah had fallen. Only Eli had remained where he was, unable to move and struggling for air as the life ebbed from him.

“Are you sure you are not badly hurt?” Joachim asked again as he spread the blanket over her legs and crawled into the buggy next to her.

“I’m still shaking inside, but I’ll be fine once we get back to your house.”

“The rain has eased. That is good.” He moved the reins, signaling Belle to start walking. The buggy creaked as the wheel came free from the mud, and the buggy moved back onto the roadway. Joachim made a sound with his mouth to encourage Belle. The mare increased her gait.

Holding the reins with one hand, Joachim wrapped his other around Sarah, pulling her close. The thought of what could have happened made his stomach sour.

She had mentioned her shaking insides. His felt no better. The shock of watching helplessly as she fell to the ground made him want to take out his frustration on Victor's friend, who had caused the mishap. If Joachim ever saw him again, he would explain the importance of giving a horse and buggy a wide berth. But would an explanation even have a small effect on the man? He seemed to be absorbed by his own needs and uncaring about the consequences of his actions to anyone else, including beautiful Sarah.

Joachim thought again of the person slumped in the rear of the car. All his instincts told him something was not right, but he did not want to alarm Sarah.

No other cars passed them on the way home, for which Joachim was grateful. He pulled Belle to a stop by the back porch and then hurried around the buggy to help Sarah down. Rebecca came out to greet them.

"I have been worried with the storm." Her frown grew more pronounced as she looked at Sarah. "Something has happened."

"Sarah fell from the buggy," he said.

"*Ach!* No!"

"A car passed us going too fast. Belle got skittish and moved off the road. There was an upward incline that caused the buggy to tilt."

"I was anything but graceful." Sarah smile ruefully.

"Did you hit your head? Perhaps you should take her to the doctor, Joachim."

Sarah held up her hand. "No to the doctor. I'm not seriously injured, just cold and a little bruised. I want to get dry and pretend that I didn't slide off a buggy seat." She glanced at Rebecca. "You were right to warn me. Riding in a buggy is not easy, especially in the rain."

"Or when cars drive too close and too fast," Rebecca added.

"The driver of the car knows Victor." Sarah touched Joachim's arm. "I keep thinking about that person sitting in the back seat. I couldn't see her through the glass. What if it *was* Miriam?"

"I am going to Victor's now. Hopefully, I will learn more about this man and his passenger."

Sarah grabbed his hand. "Be careful, Joachim. The man had an evil look in his eyes. I don't want anything to happen to you."

He wrapped his fingers through hers and stepped closer. Sarah had an effect on him that made his head swim and sent everything else into oblivion so that all he saw was her.

"I will be fine," he assured her. "Victor will wonder where I am since the rain has stopped. Besides, if he has houseguests, he will be less interested in the handyman doing repairs."

"Victor sees more than you would think. He has ways of appearing when you don't suspect him of being anywhere in the area. Be cautious, Joachim. And remember that Victor is not to be trusted."

"I will remember."

He did not want to leave Sarah, but he needed to get to the Thomin home before the next volley of rain started. If the storms continued, he would come home after working for a bit under the overhang of the porch to escape the rain.

Stepping away from her was difficult.

"Get dry and stay warm," he told her. "I will return soon."

Rebecca stood on the porch, her face drawn and looking as forlorn as Sarah. He was aware of the danger of going back to the Thomin home, but he needed to see what was happening there for himself. As Sarah had mentioned, Victor was not to be trusted. The arrival of the second man and the passenger in his car made Joachim even more concerned.

* * *

Sarah was worried about what Victor could do to Joachim. She was also worried about the man in the SUV, as well as his passenger. Could the woman be Miriam? Would her arrival at the Thomin home be a good thing or would it place her sister in even more danger? The last time Sarah had seen Miriam had been in the cabin where they had been held captive after the carjacking. Victor had claimed that a man named George had her now. If only Sarah had more information.

Rebecca and Joachim had cautioned Sarah to keep her head down, which was what she had done when the man pulled his SUV to a stop beside the buggy, yet that hadn't kept her from catching a glimpse of the guy at the wheel. He looked menacing and evil. Just like Victor. Which made her all the more concerned about her sister and worried about Joachim's safety.

Could the newcomer be George, the man who was supposed to deliver Miriam? Sarah shivered at the thought of her sister being considered a delivery, like property or chattel. This was the twenty-first century. Women weren't supposed to be owned or controlled by anyone. But life in this part of Georgia was a free-for-all with corruption run amuck. That was why she couldn't go to the police. They were corrupt, as well.

At least she had found Joachim, a man of virtue and integrity. She appreciated all he had done for her, but she worried about his safety. *Protect him, Lord,* she prayed, hoping her prayer would be heard. *And protect Miriam.*

# FIFTEEN

The ride to the Thomin property seemed especially long today, no doubt because Joachim was thinking of the way Sarah had gripped his arm and the plea he had heard in her voice.

Eventually he turned onto the Thomin driveway and guided Belle toward the barn, where she would stay while he dug through the decaying wood and replaced the rotten areas on the back porch. Once the rain stopped and the wood dried, he would paint the new patches to make them identical to the old.

The white SUV that had caused problems earlier sat parked at the front porch. Joachim stared into the rear seat, seeing nothing of interest. On the porch, he noticed a large duffel bag leaning against the side of the door frame. The arms of a man's brown dress shirt poked from the drawstring closure. Would the filled bag, if propped up in the back seat, have given the appearance of a person with long hair? He shook his head and sighed, suddenly not sure of what he had seen through the tinted windows. He flicked the reins and guided Belle around the vehicle and into the barn. After unpacking his tools from the buggy, he hurried to the back porch.

The kitchen door opened. Victor sneered. "Where have

you been? I thought you *plain* people got up early in the morning?"

As much as Joachim did not like Victor's tone, he steeled himself and gave a brief nod as he set his tools on the porch. "The storm was severe. It is dangerous to be on the road when lightning strikes so close."

"That's a lame excuse," Victor said with a wave of his hand.

"I do not offer it as an excuse" Joachim was quick to point out. "I have provided the reason I was delayed arriving. Would you prefer that I leave you now?"

Victor shook his head. "No need to get huffy."

Joachim was not huffy, but he was concerned about what might be happening inside the house. The television was tuned to a sporting channel and cheers from the crowd filtered through the back door.

"Victor, bring me a beer," a male voice demanded.

"You have guests today?" Joachim asked, glancing around Victor in hopes of seeing into the house.

"Get to work," Victor growled before he disappeared back into the kitchen.

Joachim glanced through the windows on the side of the house, searching for some sign of a woman. Seeing nothing except empty rooms, he glanced into the wooded area where Mamie mentioned the kitchen house had been located. Over the years, a thick forest had encroached within twenty feet of the Thomin home. If the kitchen house had been left standing, the woods would have surrounded the small outbuilding by now.

The sounds of the game on the television and the cheers of the onlookers bolstered Joachim's determination to continue searching. Convinced the men would remain focused on the TV, he hurried to the rear of the house.

Victor found him there. "I'm a little miffed at you,

Burkholder," he said, his voice raised. "What didn't you understand about doing a day's work?"

Joachim placed his hand on his forehead as if to shade his eyes from the sun, which had only just peered through the dark clouds.

"I wanted to see the rotting areas on the second and third stories of the house. To do so, I must stand here at the back of the structure." He eyed the upper floors and nodded. "*Yah*, there is more work to be done on the second and third floors. I can see the rot. I must go inside and open the windows to check the sills."

"Not today," Victor insisted. "We'll do it another time. Now get back to work."

Joachim complied with Victor's wishes, but he continued to peer through the windows, hoping to catch sight of the newcomer and whomever might have ridden in the rear seat. Joachim also studied the forested area in hopes of spotting some sign of the kitchen house. Victor kept appearing at the kitchen door—no doubt, checking on him. Tomorrow would be a better day. At least that was Joachim's hope.

Sarah fretted all day about Joachim and whether Miriam was at the Thomin home. Rebecca was worried as well, and both women spoke little. Instead, they busied themselves with sewing. Rebecca was piecing a quilt and taught Sarah how to cut the squares and sew them together on a treadle sewing machine. The rhythmic cadence of the machine filled the house. Sarah enjoyed the repetitive work, but the hours still dragged by too slowly, and her concerns failed to ease.

Late in the afternoon, they put away the sewing and turned to cooking the evening meal. Sarah chopped onions for a stew and almost cried, not from the acrid sting of the onions but from her own worry.

"When will Joachim get home?" she finally asked, no longer able to hold in her emotion.

"Victor will want Joachim to work until five o'clock at least," Rebecca said as she peeled carrots. "He might demand Joachim make up the hours he missed this morning due to the rain."

"Which means Joachim won't be home until after dark," Sarah said with a sigh.

A dog barked near the barn. Sarah peered from the window. "It's Angelo. He's back from his day's escapades."

"And probably hungry," Rebecca added. "Would you mind feeding him?"

"Does he ever come inside?"

Rebecca shook her head. "Dogs are creatures *Gott* created for the outdoors." She lowered her voice and looked stern as she recited the statement. Then she smiled at Sarah and returned to her usual tone of voice as she explained, "That's what my *datt* says."

"He is a gruff man?" Sarah asked.

"On the outside, *yah*, but—" Rebecca patted her heart. "On the inside, where it really matters, he is softer, although you must not tell him I said that. I think he enjoys having people think he is stern."

"And your mother?"

"*Mamm* does not let his caustic tone bother her. She is strong, but in a loving way. You will like her, Sarah."

"And what will she think of having an *Englisch* woman in the house?"

"It is not what *Mamm* thinks that concerns me. My *datt* is the one who will have questions."

"Perhaps it would be best if I leave before he and your mother return home."

"And where would you go? You said your mother has died. Your sister Miriam has disappeared, and you have lost touch with your eldest sister, Hannah. You have nowhere to call home."

"I have an aunt who supposedly lives in Willkommen. At least that's what my mother claimed, but her mind had become addled and I'm not sure if she knew what she was saying."

"I hope you can find your aunt someday."

Which seemed highly unlikely at the present time. Whether she wanted to admit it or not, Rebecca was right. Sarah had no place to call home.

She thought of the sound she had heard in the basement and wondered again if Victor was holding someone else captive. Perhaps someone who had a home and loved ones who were worried about her.

"Have you heard of anyone who has gone missing in the area?" Sarah asked.

Rebecca looked up from the carrots. "Naomi is gone if that is what you mean."

"What about other Amish women? Do you know anyone who disappeared without explanation?"

"Once, about a year ago, a man came to this house. He said he was a policeman, but he was in an unmarked vehicle and asked if we had seen a young woman named Rosie. I do not remember her last name. She was Amish and lived near Willkommen. He claimed the authorities were looking for her."

"Had Rosie done something wrong?"

"I asked, but the man said he could not say anything more." Rebecca shook her head. "He mentioned that she was Amish and had gotten mixed up with the wrong people."

Victor would fit the wrong people category. "Did you ever see her?"

"I saw a woman once at the Thomin house after Naomi was gone. That day, I had baked a cake and took it to Ms. Hazel, thinking she would be lonely without Naomi."

"That's when you saw the Amish woman?"

"*Yah*, at an upstairs window. She turned away when she saw me. I knocked on the door, but she either did not hear me or chose not to answer my knock."

"You think she could have been the missing Amish girl?"

"I wondered if she could be. Not long after that, a policeman stopped by our roadside stand and bought some of our homegrown tomatoes. I told him about the girl I had seen, but he did not seem concerned. I am not even sure if he inquired at the Thomin home. He bought three pounds of tomatoes and then did not have enough money to pay for them. He said he would come back and bring the rest of the money. I was foolish to believe him."

"You never saw him again?"

"Never."

"Joachim says I need to talk to the police."

"I do not know if that is wise," Rebecca said with a shake of her head. "The Amish do not involve law enforcement when there is a problem. We handle things ourselves. But even if we accepted the idea of contacting law enforcement, I do not believe I would trust these policemen. The Petersville police have not helped the Amish in the past."

"Victor told me the police are not to be trusted, but then that's coming from Victor."

"Yet Victor must be stopped from repeating what he did to you," Rebecca said.

"If I go back to Knoxville, I'll tell the authorities there."

Rebecca's brow raised. "Will they care what happened in the mountains of Georgia?"

"I don't know. My mother always ran from the police. When they came looking for us, it meant we had too many bills that hadn't been paid. Even before I met Victor and he told me I couldn't trust the police around here, I had a fear of anyone in law enforcement."

Rebecca patted her hand. "You have had a hard life, *yah*?"

Sarah shrugged. "I never thought of it as hard. It was my life and the only way to live that I knew. Although seeing the peace in this house shows me another way, a way I would like to follow."

"You would like to be Amish?"

"What I want is to sink roots down somewhere and have a home to call my own."

Rebecca nodded her approval. "And a good man to share that home with you as your husband?"

"You're getting ahead of me, Rebecca."

"You do not want a husband?"

"I don't want to be my mother. She made bad choices with men."

"But you are not your mother," Rebecca assured her. "You are your own person."

"A person who can't seem to stand on her own. I need to be more independent, to take care of myself and to be able to make my way in life."

Rebecca nodded. "Perhaps you yearn for a life in the world you left, instead of being holed up in an Amish house."

"The world is not what I want. I want this." She looked around her. "I want the peace and love I feel in this house. I want to work hard and have a sense of accomplishment at the end of the day."

"You have worked hard before, I can tell by the way you always help me and the way you learned to use the sewing machine so quickly today."

"But it wasn't the same in Knoxville. There was always an undercurrent of unease. I never knew if my mother would get upset and become volatile. Maybe it was the yearning for her affection, for words of acceptance that made me a hard worker—even if it never paid off. Growing up, I wanted to please her, but I always seemed to miss the mark, as the saying goes. If I tried to coax her into affirming me, she would ridicule my attempt or walk away as if she had never heard me."

"Mothers are not all the same. Some have big hearts. Others have small hearts. Hopefully, their hearts, no matter the size, are filled with love for their children."

"Yet shouldn't a mother with even a small heart, let her child know the loves she feels for that child?"

"*Yah*, it is so, but *Gott* loves you, Sarah. You are a *gut* person. You should open your heart more to Him and see if you find that acceptance for which you are searching."

Sarah wished it would be as easy as Rebecca implied.

At that moment, she heard the welcome sound of a buggy turning onto the drive and ran to the window. She smiled when she saw Joachim. She threw open the kitchen door and stepped onto the porch.

He looked tired and worried as if he carried too much on his shoulders. Sarah's heart skipped a beat as she was confronted once more with the truth. She had brought pain and struggle into Joachim's life. Anything good that she sensed in this house was there in spite of her. Yet anything that brought concern and even danger was *because* of her.

Joachim and his family had lived their years in this home and on this farm situated next to Victor's parents. All families had problems, but as far as she knew during that time, nothing had happened to upset the harmony between the Thomins and the Burkholders. Her seeing Joachim through the window at Victor's home had changed everything.

He looked at her from the buggy. Her knees became weak, and she felt light-headed. Silly reactions that didn't do anything to help Joachim. She had to control her emotions and her inner feelings. She had to guard her mind and her heart. She needed to leave the area as soon as possible because staying here, staying close to Joachim, would ruin his life.

Her spirits plummeted as she accepted the truth—leaving the peace and security she felt in this home would be the worst thing to happen to her. She had found something here. Something she wanted to hold on to, but something that didn't belong to her. Something she would only ruin if she stayed.

Her mistake. She had to leave, but leaving would break her heart.

# SIXTEEN

Joachim had not wanted to stay so late at Victor's home. He had wanted to come back to Sarah. Thoughts of her had carried him through the afternoon. Now that he was home, his heart nearly burst with joy seeing her on the porch waiting for him. If only Sarah were an Amish woman instead of a woman of the world.

Some things were not meant to be. His mother had told him that years ago when he had a crush on a non-Amish girl he had met at the lake where the teens sometimes gathered. The girl was visiting her Amish uncle and aunt, but all too soon she had returned to Atlanta, back to the life she knew. She had promised to write. He had waited for the mailman every day that summer, his heart becoming more and more saddened with each passing day he did not hear from her.

His mother's words back then brought no comfort, but they had provided the wisdom he held on to when he was on his own in North Carolina.

He had come home to find where he was meant to be, but now that he was here, all he could think about was a woman who would soon leave him. Sarah, like that young teen so long ago, would not write, and once her life returned to normal, she would probably not even remember the Amish man who had helped her escape.

"You stayed so long," Sarah said in greeting. "I was worried."

"Victor was insistent that I finish the back porch. He and the man with the scar were drinking beer as they watched sports on television all day."

"Did you see a woman with long hair?"

"I saw no one else. Now I wonder if the form in the back seat was a figment of my imagination."

Sarah furrowed her brow. "Meaning what?"

He explained about the puffy duffel bag he could have mistaken for a person.

"Oh, Joachim, I thought it could have been Miriam."

He shook his head. "I do not think there was anyone else in the house, Sarah. I am sorry."

"Did you search the woods for the kitchen house?"

"I tried, but Victor spotted me through the window and came running outside to call me back."

"Maybe he didn't want you discovering something in the woods."

"I thought he was more concerned about the work not getting done."

"What about the man with the scar?" she asked. "Did you see him?"

"*Yah*, each time he pulled another beer from the refrigerator. I wrote his license plate number on a scrap of paper. We will give it to the police."

"Not the Petersville Police—they can't be trusted. But there should be law enforcement in Willkommen. We could go there. I need to find my aunt. She may have news of Miriam."

"Yet all you know is your aunt's name."

"Isn't that enough?" Sarah asked.

"People move. They get old. She could be infirmed and receiving medical care someplace."

"Then I'll check the nursing homes. Surely there's one in the area."

"We will wait until my parents return. With Victor and the strange man next door, I do not want to leave Rebecca alone. Then I will take you."

"What about Ms. Hazel?" she asked.

"Through the kitchen window, I watched Victor fix a tray and carry it upstairs. It was probably for his mother."

"Did you see a can of rat poison in the kitchen?"

"What are you saying, Sarah?"

"I'm worried about his mother."

"You think he would poison his own mother?"

"The old rat poisons contained arsenic, which can cause lethargy, confusion. Those are all symptoms that Ms. Hazel had."

"Yet you said yourself, she is old and infirmed. She would not have to be poisoned to appear confused or dazed."

"Except she was caring for herself while Naomi was there if what Levi said is true. I got the impression Naomi was more of a housekeeper than a caregiver."

"I do not doubt Levi."

"Nor do I, but it seems suspicious to me that Ms. Hazel's health would fail so quickly."

"Naomi has been gone for almost a year. Many things can change in a year. Ms. Hazel could have had a stroke. She could have gotten pneumonia, which would cause serious complications and setbacks."

"And she could be ingesting small doses of arsenic," Sarah said again.

"What about the sleeping pills we found in her dresser drawer?"

"I'm not counting those out either. Victor might give

her sleeping pills so she will stay in bed while he drives round the countryside looking for women."

"And if he had someone holed up in the basement, why would he not use that person to help with his mother?"

From the look on her face, Joachim's statement had stopped Sarah like a brick wall. Surely she realized he was right.

"Why would Victor lock someone in an underground cellar if he needed care for his infirmed mother?" Joachim asked again.

Sarah raked her hand through her hair, nearly knocking off her bonnet. She caught it before it dropped to the ground. Strands of her hair pulled loose and fell over her cheek. He reached out his hand to weave them back in place.

"I don't seem to be getting the hang of this Amish thing, Joachim."

She was being truthful, and he knew it. Sarah was not suited for the Amish life. She needed her world and not his.

"Sometimes we want what cannot be."

She stared into his eyes for a long moment. "The problem is, Joachim, I'm not sure what I want."

With a heavy sigh, she walked to the door, pushed it open and slipped back inside.

Joachim felt as confused as Sarah seemed to be. Surely she realized they were not meant for each other. No matter how much he wanted what could never be.

Sarah entered the kitchen and washed her hands, then seeing the pot of boiled potatoes in the sink, she grabbed the potato masher and took out her frustration on the spuds. By the time Joachim stepped inside, the pot was filled with creamy mashed potatoes that would be a perfect side dish to the roast Rebecca was cooking in the oven. The rich aromas filled the kitchen and made Sarah's mouth water.

She refused to look at Joachim and then hated herself for being so petty. He was thinking of her safety and was trying to be cautious. If the Amish didn't trust the Petersville police, there had to be a good reason, but Joachim was right. They needed law enforcement somewhere to run the license plate and then investigate whether the man with the scar had anything to do with Miriam.

Ever since Victor had turned against her in the attic the day she had escaped, Sarah had wondered if she would ever see her sister again. For all she knew, Miriam might be dead. Something Sarah was not able to admit aloud.

Tears sprang to her eyes, but she blinked them aside. She had to be strong and hold on to the hope that Miriam was alive. If so, Sarah had to find her.

Again she thought of the scratching sound in the basement. Suppose Miriam was being held captive in some other place and had tried to alert others to her whereabouts. What if her signal for help had been ignored? Miriam wasn't in Victor's basement, but if some other woman was being held captive, Sarah had to act.

Joachim entered the kitchen and stood for a long moment just inside the door, staring at her.

Sarah's heart ached. "I have to find the kitchen house. If my sister was being held in a place like that, I'd want someone to try to save her. I can't stay here in safety when someone might be locked away in an underground cellar."

"I will go tonight," Joachim said. "When it is dark and when Victor's friend is gone or has passed out from his drinking. You will stay here with Rebecca."

"No, Joachim. I'm going with you. I have to go. I can't save my sister, but maybe I can save someone else. Sometimes we have to sacrifice for another. Isn't that what your faith teaches you? It's what I believe. Christ gave up his life so we might be saved. Surely you believe that, too. So you have to understand why I need to go with you."

"What if I don't go?" he asked.

"Then I will go alone. Either way, I have to make sure no one else is trapped in Victor's snare."

"And if something happens to you, Sarah. What will happen to me?"

"The same thing that will happen when I leave here. You will go on with your life." She glanced around the kitchen. "Your future is here with your family. I have to make a new life for myself, but I would not be able to go on if I didn't find that root cellar and determine if someone is being held there."

She looked at him. "Can you understand?"

He nodded. "*Yah*, I understand. But it puts you in more danger, which is not what I want. I want something more for you, Sarah."

"Then go with me, Joachim. We'll find the kitchen house and search for someone held against her will. Then when I leave Petersville, I'll know I did the right thing."

"What about Ms. Hazel?"

"I'll alert the authorities in Willkommem or the next town or Atlanta if need be. I'll keep talking to law enforcement until someone listens to me. That's what Miriam would do." She grabbed the pitcher of milk and poured some into the potatoes, then mixed in a large scoop of butter.

As good as the mashed potatoes appeared and as wonderful as the smells were in the kitchen, Sarah suddenly wasn't hungry. Everything was about to change. Joachim's parents would return soon, and they wouldn't want an *Englisch* woman underfoot, which made Sarah sad.

For all her bluster, she didn't want to leave this Amish home. Even more important, she didn't want to leave Joachim.

# SEVENTEEN

Joachim tapped on Sarah's bedroom door. "It is time," he whispered, hearing her stir. He turned on the flashlight as she opened the door.

"I fell asleep," she admitted, rubbing her face.

"Are you sure you want to do this?"

"We discussed it earlier. I have to, Joachim. I appreciate you going with me."

"I told you that I would go alone. I had hoped to search the woods today, but Victor kept too close of a watch. He seemed nervous, like a skittish colt."

"Maybe his friend frightens him. The guy looked like he was used to pushing his weight around."

"He is a big man, *yah*. I do not even want to think what happened that caused his scar."

"Perhaps too many beers in a bar someplace."

Joachim held his laughter in check so as not to wake Rebecca. "Let's hope both he and Victor are sleeping off their beers and will not arise from their slumber."

"I'd like to feed both men those sleeping pills we found in Ms. Hazel's room. Then they wouldn't hear us as we search the property."

"We will find the kitchen house tonight," Joachim assured her. "Tomorrow we can determine how to help Ms. Hazel."

She glanced at the small arch of light. "You brought a flashlight instead of a candle. Thank you, Joachim."

"The flashlight will help us find the root cellar."

He stretched out his hand and was grateful when she placed hers in his. Her skin was soft and smooth, and her nearness made his heart skip a beat. He needed to control his emotions tonight lest he do something foolish that might alert someone in the Thomin house.

Sarah's safety was the most important thing to him. Actually, if truth be known, it was all that mattered.

"We will take the path through the woods on foot," Joachim whispered when they left the house and headed along the drive. "The buggy would make too much noise. Stay behind me on the trail. I must turn off the flashlight so Victor does not see us. The trees will block the light from the stars, forcing us to move slowly."

They made their way along the narrow path. Joachim had traveled it many times in daylight. Tonight, the sounds of the forest seemed especially ominous. Leaves rustled, perhaps from a squirrel or some night creature crawling through the underbrush. Snakes were common, but he would not mention that complication to Sarah.

"Wait, Joachim," she whispered. "My skirt caught on a bush."

She tugged it free and then headed on. "It's so dark."

He squeezed her hand. "We are almost there."

Except the trail seemed to stretch forever.

Eventually, they came to the edge of the tree line, where Joachim stopped. He put his finger to his lips as a reminder for them to remain quiet.

For a long moment he studied the house and surrounding area, then motioned Sarah to follow him. Slowly they wove behind the outbuildings and the barn.

"We will cut through the trees until we get to the area where the kitchen house should be located."

Sarah glanced at the Thomin home. "All the windows are dark. Victor used to leave a small light on in Ms. Hazel's room. When I took breakfast to her in the morning, it would still be on."

Joachim squeezed her hand again, hoping to provide reassurance. "We must stay focused. Tonight we will find the kitchen house and determine what caused the sound you heard. As I mentioned, we will decide how to help Ms. Hazel tomorrow."

She nodded. Even with the darkness, he could see her eyes, wide with worry.

"Do you see the SUV that belongs to the man with the scar?" she asked.

"No, but it was parked in front of the house earlier. We would not be able to see it from here. As much as he drank today, I hope he did not try to drive home."

"He's probably staying in one of the guest bedrooms on the second floor. Victor's bedroom faces the front of the house, but the windows in the guest room overlook the back lawn. We need to be careful in case he happens to wake."

"He won't see us, Sarah."

Joachim took the lead. Without a path to follow, he had to pick his way through the underbrush.

"Be careful," he cautioned as he navigated an especially thick area of bramble.

If only he had been able to search the woods in the light of day. Tonight, everything lay in shadows so that even the most common tree or shrub took on a strange appearance.

At long last they arrived in the area where the kitchen house most likely would have been located. Joachim stared into the darkness, seeing nothing.

"What do we do now?" Sarah asked, leaning closer.

"We start searching and walk in a grid fashion so we cover all the ground to make sure we don't miss any trace of it. Remember, it might have been torn down, or fallen apart due to disrepair. But hopefully, we will find some sign of an older structure."

"And if we don't?" Sarah asked.

"Then we will return home without any answer to your question about the noise in the basement."

"I don't want to give up, Joachim."

"I do not want that either. Let us walk next to each other so we can cover two times the amount of area," he suggested.

She glanced over her shoulder at the large Thomin house. "The windows in one of the guest bedrooms are open. That may be where Victor's friend is staying."

Joachim put his finger to his lips. "Then we will be quiet so he has nothing to hear."

He grabbed her hand. "Come, we must walk."

Traversing the area in the dark was a challenge. The smallest bush or tree root caused Sarah to stumble. Joachim caught her each time and helped her regain her balance.

"I'm beginning to think this is impossible," she admitted.

"We will keep looking. Do not get discouraged."

"It's not that."

"You are tired."

She nodded. "You must be, too. I keep thinking about the scratching sound and whether Miriam is being held someplace far from here."

"We can go home and return tomorrow," Joachim offered.

"No. I want to keep searching."

They walked in silence for the next fifteen minutes.

Sarah stopped to lean against a tree. "I'm sorry, Joachim. You would do better without me."

"We will leave now."

Her shoulders slumped. "I feel like a failure."

"You are no such thing. You are tired and still not strong enough. Do not be discouraged."

"Maybe just another ten minutes," she suggested.

He nodded, and they set out again. A break in the trees surprised them. The clear area was easier to navigate with the stars visible overhead, which shed light on the ground.

Joachim pointed to a raised area just a few steps away. They hurried forward and then stopped to stare at what appeared to be stacked bricks.

"It looks like part of an old chimney," he said. "We have found the kitchen house—or at least what remains of it."

He glanced around, searching for some sign of a root cellar or opening for a tunnel. If only they had more light. Glancing over his shoulder, he saw the big house through the trees. They were close to finding what they came searching for, but would the remains of the old structure reveal anything about the scratching sounds Sarah had heard, namely whether a person was being held captive?

Sarah's heart pounded with excitement and anticipation. They'd found at least a portion of the old kitchen house. And even though the building was mostly gone, surely the tunnel had remained. Now they needed to find what was buried belowground.

"No telling how much dirt and debris has settled over this area," she said, glancing around.

"We will walk a few steps away from the chimney," Joachim suggested. "Perhaps ten or twelve feet, and then walk around the periphery of what would have been the outbuilding."

"That sounds like a good plan." They paced off the steps, and then each turned in opposite directions. Sarah walked to the left and took tiny steps, her gaze on the ground. Knowing they had discovered the location of the actual kitchen house gave her confidence. Her foot stumbled over a raised area. She bent and touched the rock that had caught her foot.

"I've found the foundation for a wall," she whispered to Joachim.

He hurried to join her. "*Gut.* We will keep walking, hopefully around the outer wall of the old structure."

Together, they slowly moved forward. Sometimes the stone wall disappeared, but they continued on until they found another section of the old wall.

When they were almost three-quarters of the way around, Sarah stopped. "What's that?" she asked, pointing to a metal slab on the ground.

Joachim bent and worked his hands over the flat surface then down the edge of the covering. "I have found a padlock."

Sarah's heart raced. "It's the door to the cellar."

Joachim nodded. "You are right."

He glanced at the house that sat less than fifty feet away. "If only the windows in the house were not opened. If we are going to explore the tunnel, then I will need to break the lock, which will make noise."

"We don't have a choice, Joachim. We can't turn back now."

"*Yah*, it is true. We must continue our search." He pulled a hammer from his waistband and knelt on the ground next to the metal slab.

Hammer in hand, he glanced up at her. "If you hear anyone coming, run through the woods and angle around, keeping the barn as a point of reference. It will be dark so you will need to be careful, but you should find the path back to my farm on the far side of the barn."

"You're worrying me."

"That is because I am worried, Sarah."

"If Victor and his buddy are sleeping off all the beer they drank, the sound of the hammer might not wake them."

"This we can only hope to be true. Let me know if you see anything change at the house."

She stared at the windows, dark and devoid of life.

Joachim raised the hammer.

She held her breath.

Her heart jerked as his hammer hit the padlock. The clank of metal striking metal echoed through the forest, shattering the night and the stillness.

Sarah continued to stare at the windows. Would she be able to see anyone as dark as it was?

She glanced down. The padlock was still attached. Joachim raised his hammer and struck again.

A light went on in the house.

"Joachim?" She pointed to the window.

He fiddled with the padlock and then held it up triumphantly. Quickly, he stepped aside, grabbed the edge of the metal door and lifted it open.

They both stared into a dark hole.

"Watch the house," Joachim whispered. "Run if someone comes outside, but warn me first. I am going down into the cellar."

She grabbed his arm. "Be careful."

He nodded. Pulling out his flashlight, he stepped onto the wooden stairway that led into the darkness.

Sarah's heart lurched. She wrung her hands, wishing she and Joachim could be anyplace else except at this root cellar in the middle of the night.

She focused her eyes on the light in the window. The minutes passed too slowly. Leaves rustled behind her. She glanced back, half expecting to see Victor. Relieved when he didn't appear, she bent and stared into the darkness.

"Joachim?" she whispered.

Her heart pounded. The sound of her pulse roared in her ears. Where was Joachim and what had he found?

From out of the darkness down the tunnel, a face appeared. Not Joachim's, but a young woman.

Slender, pale, wide-eyed.

Sarah stretched out her hand and helped the woman up the stairs. Tears glistened on her dirt-smudged cheeks. She pulled in a ragged breath. Sarah's heart broke thinking of what she had endured.

"I'm Sarah." She opened her arms and pulled the woman into her embrace.

"My...my name is Rosie Glick."

Sarah smiled. "You're safe now. Victor won't hurt you again."

Rosie gripped her tightly for a long moment and then turned as Joachim climbed from the cellar.

He held a pile of blankets in his arms. Rosie hurried forward and took the blankets from him, a look of relief on her slender face.

Sarah stepped closer. Her heart bursting with wonder and surprise as she stared down, seeing the tiny newborn infant in Rosie's arms.

# EIGHTEEN

"We must hurry," Joachim warned both women. He lowered the metal covering into place and motioned them to head deeper into the woods, away from the house.

A door slammed.

"Victor?"

A man stood in the backyard, the big guy they had seen in the car. He called out for Victor a second time and then started jogging toward them.

"Hurry," Joachim whispered.

Rosie clutched the baby and tried to keep up. Joachim grabbed Rosie's arm. Together, he and Sarah helped the young woman move faster.

Joachim glanced over his shoulder.

The darkness prevented him from seeing the man, but he heard his heavy footfalls.

Again the visitor called out for Victor.

Joachim would not let Rosie be captured again, especially with the baby.

The barn appeared on the right. If only they could clear the outbuildings and find the path.

A kitchen light flicked on in the house, and a person stepped onto the back porch. Shoulder-length brown hair, medium height, slender build.

Sarah stopped and stared at the figure. Her eyes narrowed. "Miriam?"

Joachim turned just as Sarah started to run, not away from the big house, but toward it.

He pointed out the barn to Rosie. "Wait there with the baby."

Joachim hurried to cut Sarah off before Victor's friend saw her. Thankfully, he caught up to her and grabbed her arm.

She turned on him, anger flashing from her eyes. "It's my sister. I have to save her."

"Look again, Sarah. What you see is a man with shoulder-length hair. Your eyes are playing tricks on you."

She shook her head and glanced again at the slender, but very masculine, figure on the porch. "Oh no," she groaned, realizing her mistake.

Joachim took her hand. "Come. We must hurry."

They started to run, but not toward the barn. Joachim did not want to lead the men to Rosie. Instead, he turned back the way they had come.

Victor's friend chased after them. The long-haired man, as well. Sarah gasped for air. Her foot caught and she stumbled. Joachim helped her up. She was winded and frightened. The big man with the scar was gaining on them, his friend lagging some steps behind.

Joachim's heart pounded, fearing Sarah would be captured again. He would rather die himself than let that happen, but she could run no farther, which meant they had to hide. But where?

*Think! Think!*

"Go on without me, Joachim."

He wrapped his arm around her shoulders and guided her deeper into the underbrush. Both men followed too close behind them.

"It's no use," Sarah gasped.

She was right. Running would not work.

The clearing appeared ahead. "Hurry, Sarah. Just a little farther."

*Gott, help us*, he prayed.

Dark clouds filled the night sky, blocking the starlight and making the clearing even more difficult to traverse. They were close. He knew it, but the men were close, too, gaining on them.

Joachim stumbled. He stopped short and dropped to the ground.

"What's wrong?" Sarah cried.

His fingers found what he had been looking for. He lifted the metal slab, exposing the black void.

"Hurry, Sarah, crawl into the cellar."

"No, I can't."

"You have to. Now." He took her hand and ushered her forward. "I will not leave you. We will hide together until the men return to the house."

"But—"

"Now, Sarah." The men's footfalls echoed in the night. They were close. So. Very. Close.

With a faint whimper, Sarah climbed down the wooden stairs and disappeared into the darkness. Joachim followed her. He lowered the slab over them. The musty scent of the damp earth filled his nostrils. Sarah grabbed his arm. He pulled her close, feeling her body tremble as the men ran across the clearing, searching for them.

"I will not leave you." Sarah kept playing Joachim's words over in her head as they waited silently for Victor's friends to give up their search and return to the house. Her head rested against Joachim's chest. She heard his heartbeat, which calmed her racing pulse and helped her endure the time they remained underground.

Finally, Joachim stirred. "I'm going to raise the covering ever so slightly. Do not make a sound."

He moved away from her. A lump filled her throat, and she blinked back tears that burned her eyes. She had to be brave and remain still. At least she was with Joachim. Her heart went out to Rosie, who was alone with her baby. Just so the men wouldn't find her.

A gust of fresh air floated over Sarah as Joachim pushed up on the metal slab. She could see the outline of his profile as he stared motionless through the opening.

Finally, he nodded and reached for her hand. "The house is dark. I trust they have gone back to bed."

Together they climbed from the cellar. Sarah sucked in a deep breath of fresh cool air, grateful to be free. Joachim replaced the covering over the root cellar and pointed toward the barn.

Slowly, they moved away from the house. If they only would find Rosie and her baby waiting for them.

Sarah glanced back at the house that stood black against the night. She recalled the men who had chased them—the large, scarred man they had met on the road, and the other man who she had mistaken for her sister. The slender man with shoulder-length brown hair had been the passenger in the SUV and not Miriam. Just as Joachim had said, her eyes had played tricks on her. Another mistake. She had made so many.

Joachim squeezed her hand as if he could read her mind. He pointed to a path through the woods that allowed them to move more quickly.

Her heart pounded as they approached the barn and entered through a side door.

"Rosie?" Joachim called, his voice little more than a whisper.

Silence.

He walked by the stalls and peered into the nooks and crevices. Had Victor or one of the other men found her and taken her back to the house?

Sarah wanted to scream with frustration and anger at herself. If she hadn't made the mistake about Miriam, Rosie and her baby would have escaped.

*Oh, God, help her!*

A soft mewing made Sarah turn. She glanced through the open doorway to a second outbuilding. There on the ground, with her back against the wall, sat Rosie, holding the baby in her arms.

Rosie was exhausted, and the trip back to Joachim's house sapped what little strength she had.

"Only a little farther," Sarah whispered, taking the baby and cuddling the infant close. Joachim picked Rosie up in his arms and carried her back to his house.

Sarah knocked on the kitchen door and Rebecca let them in. "Where have you been? I heard you leave the house, and I have been so worried not knowing what happened."

Joachim carried Rosie inside. Rebecca guided him to the rocker by the fire. "It is warm here. I will make tea."

She hurried to the kitchen and passed Sarah, only now noticing the bundle in her arms. Rebecca stopped short.

"Oh my, Sarah. Do you have what I think you have?"

She nodded. "Rosie's baby."

Rebecca turned to look at her brother. "Victor was holding her captive?"

Joachim nodded. "In the morning, I will go to Petersville. The police need to be told. If one officer is corrupt and not interested in getting involved, then I will find another one who will listen. And if not Petersville, then I will drive to Willkommen. Victor must be stopped. He must be stopped now."

Sarah's heart soared with emotion as she rocked the baby who slept in her arms. She had never held a baby so small or so beautiful.

Rebecca prepared food for Rosie, who ate and then asked for more. She kept looking at Sarah and making sure her baby was still sleeping.

No one asked her questions. There would be time for that later. Right now, she appeared too tired and had been through so much.

"There's a spare room upstairs and a bed," Sarah said. "We'll care for the baby down here while you get some sleep."

"Are you sure?" Rosie asked.

Sarah nodded. "Tell me his name."

"Joseph. My baby's name is Joseph."

"Don't worry about your little one," Sarah assured her. "Get the rest you need. Tomorrow we can talk."

Rosie gave a weak smile. "Thank you for saving Joseph and me."

"I heard scratching on the wall when I was in the basement of the big house. That was you, wasn't it?"

Rosie nodded, her face still so pale. "Victor locked me in the root cellar, but he did not remember the tunnel."

"How did you find it?"

"I searched for some way to get out and found the doorway. Dirt had piled up around it. Before the baby came, I cleared the dirt and pried open the door."

"You went into the tunnel?"

Rosie nodded. "Victor left a candle for me. I used that to see my way. I thought it would lead to an exit. When I got to the end and found it blocked, I cried." She glanced at the baby. "That night, my pains started."

"You went into labor and delivered the baby by yourself?"

Rosie nodded, then closed her eyes.

The memory was either too difficult or the young woman too fatigued to go on.

"You need to rest," Sarah insisted. "Tomorrow we will decide what to do next. You are from around here?"

"My parents live near Willkommen."

Sarah glanced at Joachim. If he took Rosie and her baby home to her parents, perhaps Sarah could go with them and make inquiries about her aunt.

Before she could mention her plan to Joachim, he headed to the door.

"Stay here with Rebecca and Rosie," he told Sarah. "I will go back along the path and make certain we were not followed."

Her heart lurched. "Oh, Joachim, be careful. Victor is a terrible man, and his friends seem equally as bad. I'm afraid of what could happen to you if they see you. Please, don't go," she pleaded.

"It is important to stay on guard, Sarah. This is what I must do."

"But suppose you find them. You don't have a weapon. Your faith does not allow you to respond to their violence."

"Sometimes a man must do what he knows he must do."

"Which means you could get hurt."

"When I was working in North Carolina, I was forced to confront two men who thought being Amish meant being weak. They had no love for *Gott* in their hearts, Sarah, and they left me no alternative but to protect that which was mine."

"What do you mean?"

"I had to show them the fallacy of their ways. Did not Christ drive the money changers from the temple?"

She nodded. "Would your minister approve of your actions?"

"We do not have a minister, Sarah. A bishop leads us and he, more than likely, did not approve of me leaving my home. For a period of time, I had my feet in both worlds, trying to be both Amish and *Englisch*. For that, I must ask forgiveness."

Sarah didn't understand how one man could hold so much power over Joachim. "And what if the bishop says you cannot stay in the area?"

"If I ask forgiveness of *Gott* and of my Amish community, he will not deny my request. He wants what *Gott* wants, and that is for me to live by the *Ordnung*, the rules established for our community."

"What does the *Ordnung* say about matters of the heart?"

His brow furrowed. "A man takes a wife and the two become one. This is the way we have lived through the years. Perhaps I do not understand your question?"

"What if the woman is not a member of the Amish faith?"

Joachim lowered his gaze and sighed. "Then the relationship could not continue. An Amish man marries an Amish woman. Marriage to someone outside the faith is not allowed."

"Isn't that narrow-minded, Joachim?"

He shook his head. "It is the way we keep our faith and our way of life. As much as I tried, I could not walk on both sides of the fence. The choice must be made, either to fully embrace the Amish faith or to leave it altogether. A person must decide which way he or she is to live life." He smiled weakly. "Sometimes that is a hard choice."

Then he turned and walked to the door. After grabbing his hat off the wall peg, he reached for the knob.

Cool nighttime air blew into the kitchen as the door opened, making Sarah shiver. Joachim had clearly explained the choices available to a person drawn to the Amish way of life. Where did Sarah stand?

She was attracted to Joachim and, as she suddenly realized, to his faith, as well. Although she wasn't ready to fully embrace the *plain* life. She needed longer to consider her options, but she was running out of time. Remain *Englisch* and say goodbye to Joachim, or embrace his Amish faith and remain in the area. If only she knew what the future would hold.

She glanced though the window, seeing Joachim hurry toward the pathway. She was running out of time.

Amish or *Englisch*? The decision was one she wasn't able to make. At least not tonight.

# NINETEEN

Less than three hours later, the first rays of dawn pulled Sarah from a light slumber. The baby was still asleep in her arms. She glanced around the room, hoping to find Joachim in one of the chairs. Instead, she realized, with a heaviness in her heart, that she was alone.

Too much time had passed since he had left the house. Thoughts of what could have happened stabbed her like a knife. A tiny cry escaped her lips, making the infant stir.

She rocked the little one and tried to force the vision of Joachim being locked in the attic room from her mind. Even worse were visions of him thrown into the dark, dank root cellar.

If Victor was holding him captive, then she couldn't let him remain there. She had to do something to set him free. But what and how?

The baby stretched, then wrinkled his precious face and started to root for a feeding. She patted and rocked, hoping to soothe him back to sleep, yet little Joseph continued to search for nourishment. A shrill cry escaped his thin lips.

As much as she didn't want to wake Rosie, the baby was hungry and needed to be fed. His cries quickly became inconsolable. Sarah carried him upstairs. The door to the extra bedroom jerked open, and Rosie stretched out her arms to take the child. The baby nestled against his mother.

She nodded her thanks to Sarah and then retreated into the bedroom and closed the door behind her.

Sarah stood in the hallway and longed to hold the baby in her arms again. The unconditional love she had felt for the small infant surprised her. A love without reservation. The little one had accepted her love unconditionally as well, and had slept in her arms with absolute trust.

Sarah had always wanted that type of love from her own mother. Instead, she had received criticism and scolding and had grown up sensing she was unwanted. If Sarah ever had children, she would ensure they knew how much she loved each of them and how special they were to her.

She sighed and shook her head, surprised by thoughts of children when she had never allowed herself to consider marriage and family. Surely it was this house with the love and acceptance she had found here that was changing her mind.

But Joachim had told her without hesitation that he could not be interested in an *Englisch* woman. She did not need to be told twice. He had made his feelings on the matter perfectly clear. With all that had happened and as confused as her life had been, she wasn't ready to commit to the Amish faith. At least, not yet.

A swell of melancholy filled her as she headed back downstairs. She walked slowly through the house, seeing the simple beauty of the rockers by the wood stove, the calendar hanging on the wall in the kitchen, and the gas lights sitting on stands in front of aluminum disks that magnified the light and helped to brighten the rooms. She still had an aversion to matches, but the long-necked fireplace lighters and the gas lights with tall hurricane chimneys that encircled the flames were no longer threatening.

She ran her hand over the silky smooth wood of the dry sink and marveled at the workmanship. Had Joachim made the piece for his mother perhaps? Or had his father, who Joachim claimed was a farmer at heart, crafted the kitchen work area long ago for his new bride?

She stepped to the window, seeing the warm glow of the first light on the horizon. The barnyard came into view. As she watched, a small animal bounded along the drive and raced toward the house. Sarah hurried onto the porch and bent to welcome Angelo home.

"Oh, it's good to see you, boy." She scratched his neck. The pup nosed at Sarah's hands and jumped to lick her face. She laughed at his excitement and attention, and again, she was filled with a sense of acceptance and love.

Footsteps sounded. Her heart skidded to a halt. She stood, ready to flee into the house, but before she did so, her eyes caught sight of the man walking toward her.

Her heart went from a standstill to an erratic thumping that warmed her neck and made her want to run to welcome this man home.

"Oh, Joachim," she said as he drew closer. "I was so worried about you."

He opened his arms and reached for her. She stepped into his embrace, the thoughts of their differences fleeing so that all that mattered was being with him.

"The night is over, Sarah, and we are both safe."

She lifted her face to his, longing to remain forever in his arms. He lowered his lips to hers, but before they kissed, a car turned into the drive and captured both of them in the arc of its headlights.

Sarah raised her hand to her forehead, shielding her eyes from the glare as the vehicle pulled to a stop.

A man stepped to the ground. "Joachim Burkholder?"

Sarah felt Joachim tense. *"Yah?"*

The man moved to the front of the car, his dark blue uniform now visible in the headlights.

Sarah blinked and saw the logo for the Petersville Police Department on the side of the car.

"I'm here to take you into headquarters for questioning," the officer said. "You're wanted in connection with the death of Eli Burkholder."

"What?" Sarah looked from the policeman to Joachim.

Shock registered on his face. "Eli died five years ago."

"Did you not flee the area immediately after his death without leaving the statement that law enforcement specifically requested?"

"I do not remember being told to do that."

"Maybe you'll remember more clearly if you come down to headquarters."

"This is not something I want to do."

"Are you resisting arrest, sir?"

Resisting arrest? Everything was going from bad to worse. At first the policeman had mentioned questioning Joachim. Now he talked about making an arrest.

"You've made a mistake," Sarah insisted. "Joachim has done nothing wrong. You need to question Victor Thomin. He's at his mother's house. It's the next property on the road to Petersville. The turn is about a mile and a half from here."

"Ma'am, the Thomins are one of the oldest and most respected families in this area."

"I'm not disparaging the family, I'm talking about their son, Victor. He—"

Joachim grabbed her hand. "Sarah, be quiet. This is not the time."

Rebecca stepped onto the porch. "Joachim, what is happening?"

"Go inside," Joachim insisted. He glanced at Sarah. "Both of you."

"Why do you want to question him?" Sarah demanded of the officer.

"Lady, we received a tip that Mr. Burkholder was in town. We've been wanting to talk to him for years about that old investigation. And now that he's back, he has also been incriminated in illegal operations happening in this local area that involves human trafficking."

"If you're investigating human trafficking, then you definitely have the wrong man. I told you to question Victor Thomin," Sarah insisted, but the officer ignored her and moved to handcuff Joachim.

"I will go peacefully," he told the cop.

The officer ushered him to the squad car, where he frisked him and then clicked the handcuffs into place.

Seeing Joachim handled like a common criminal made Sarah shake inwardly. What was happening? Her world was falling apart. Victor was the kind of man who should be taken in for questioning, not Joachim.

Rebecca hurried from the porch to stand next to Sarah. Both women watched the officer open the rear door of the squad car and shove Joachim into the back seat. The door slammed shut, sending a shiver down Sarah's spine.

The officer climbed behind the wheel, started his car and backed onto the main road. The police sedan turned toward Petersville and drove off.

The stillness was overpowering. Sarah stared at the road as the taillights disappeared from sight.

Angelo nuzzled Sarah's leg and then started to howl.

Joachim glanced back through the window of the police squad car and caught a last glimpse of Sarah standing in the drive, her eyes wide and fear wrapped around her slender face.

After what she had just heard, he was certain she

thought he was a killer, just like the heinous man who had killed her mother.

Any chance of convincing her that the Amish way of life—and particularly life with him—would be something she should consider had disappeared the moment the police officer had clasped the cuffs around his wrists.

The night of the buggy accident, Joachim's world had fallen apart. In the years since, he had tried to rebuild it, but all his efforts had fallen apart in the last few moments. He felt vile and unwanted, like a snake that needed to be squashed underfoot lest its deadly venom strike someone down. He had looked into Sarah's eyes and seen her gaze go from one of affection to disgust.

Moments earlier, he had come so close to kissing her that he could almost feel her sweet lips on his. His heart had soared as high as the eagle flies, and he had thought of nothing else except holding her close and keeping her safely protected and with him for the rest of his life.

Then everything had plummeted and his future, the one he had envisioned with Sarah at his side, disappeared with the click of the cuffs.

Thoughts of going to prison and all the humiliation that accompanied incarceration ate at his gut. Surely he would be exonerated of guilt, yet even the accusation of wrongdoing would mark him. He shook his head, seeing another option, one that was also troubling. He envisioned the loneliness of a vagabond carpenter traveling from job to job, never with a place to call home and never with a *gut* woman like Sarah—no, not a *gut* woman, an amazing woman—to walk with him through life.

The officer was talking on the radio, unaware of the pain Joachim was experiencing. Would he realize his mistake, or would Joachim be held behind bars and forced to face a trial where he would be accused of being responsible for his brother's death?

Perhaps his father had been right. Joachim did not deserve to remain part of the family. He had been shunned and rightfully so.

Gott, *forgive my transgressions. I came home to reconcile with my datt. That reconciliation will never be.*

He turned again to glance back at the farm where he had grown up and where he and Sarah had shared such a short period of time. He now knew what he wanted in life. He wanted his Amish faith, and he wanted Sarah walking through life next to him.

This morning, riding in the back of the police car, Joachim realized he had wanted too much.

# TWENTY

Sarah's heart was heavy as she returned to the house and climbed the stairs without saying anything to Rebecca. Joachim, with his concern for others and his willingness to help those in need, was not a man who would take a person's life. Nor did he have anything to do with trafficking. Sarah couldn't believe such nonsense, yet she herself had watched as he had been handcuffed and locked in the back of a patrol car.

Joachim, who had come to her rescue, who had saved her from Victor, who looked at her and made her knees weak and her stomach turn to jelly, was the most wonderful man she had ever known, yet she couldn't stay around and hope there was a chance for them. Joachim had said as much himself when he had discussed the differences between them.

Sarah was an *Englischer.*

Joachim was Amish.

And never the two shall meet or mix or fall in love or declare their love or get married and have a family.

His arrest had nothing to do with her upset. Even if the police officer had not appeared, Sarah would still be struggling to make levelheaded decisions about what to do next. How foolish she had been to have given her heart to Joachim. He wasn't meant for her. After all the legal problems were ironed out, Joachim would find a wonderful Amish woman who would cook his food and sew his clothes and help him in the fields and with milking the cows and slaughtering the pigs. All the things about which Sarah knew nothing. Although she was willing to learn.

She lightened her footsteps when she passed Rosie's room and headed to her own chamber. Pushing open the door, she stepped inside and then quietly closed the door behind her.

The tension that had welled up within her since she had been in Joachim's arms burst loose. Tears fell from her eyes. She stumbled to the bed and collapsed onto the thick quilt as she struggled to control her outburst. She didn't want to concern Rosie or Rebecca with her tears. Hopefully, they wouldn't hear her when she left the house. She could no longer stay here, where everything reminded her of Joachim.

But where would she go and what would she do? A trip to Willkommen to inquire about her aunt? Yes, that made sense as a first step. If the woman couldn't be found, Sarah would board a bus and return to Knoxville.

She wiped the tears from her eyes, and in spite of the heaviness of her heart, she eventually fell asleep. Awakening a few hours later, Sarah headed downstairs and hurried into the kitchen. Rosie sat at the table sipping from a mug of coffee.

"Did you sleep?" Sarah asked.

"Not with the baby in bed with me. I had slept earlier, but after he nursed, I kept wondering how I would face my parents."

"They love you, Rosie. They want you home with them." At least that's what Sarah hoped.

She poured a cup of coffee, weighing how she would

leave this wonderful Amish home and how she would get to Willkommen to find her aunt.

"Joachim had said he would take me home," Rosie said. "Now I'm not sure how I will get there."

Sarah nodded. "Perhaps I will go with you, Rosie. I need to find an aunt who may live in Willkommen."

"You are not staying here with Rebecca and Joachim?"

*Joachim isn't here*, Sarah wanted to remind her. Instead, she asked, "How long did you help Ms. Hazel?"

"More than seven months."

"You didn't try to escape?"

"Where would I go? I was an unwed mother. I could not go home. I could not go anywhere."

"What about Joseph's father?"

"His name was William." Rosie lowered her eyes. "William is dead."

"I'm so sorry." Sarah's heart went out to the young woman. "For those reasons you never tried to escape?"

"That is true, although if I had known that Victor would lock me in the root cellar close to my delivery time, I would have tried to escape. He was not abusive except with his words, but I was foolish to think he was a better man than he proved himself to be."

"What led to him forcing you into the cellar?"

"I told him the baby was due, and that I needed help. He did not want to bring in a midwife. It was easier to lock me away than to have a doctor or midwife find out he was holding me in his mother's house."

"How did Ms. Hazel seem when you first arrived?"

"She was sick, and her condition grew worse. I told Victor she needed to see a doctor. He refused to take her. Instead, he gave her sleeping pills."

"You saw him give her pills?"

"*Yah*, many times."

"You need to tell the police."

Rosie shook her head. "I do not want to talk to the police. They cannot be trusted. You must know this for yourself. After all, they have Joachim. From the window, I watched as the officer put him in the police car."

Sarah's heart ached, thinking of Joachim in custody. She had run away from law enforcement as a child each time her mother woke her in the middle of the night, saying they must leave town before the police came knocking at their door.

She had vowed to never live like that again. She didn't trust law enforcement, but she wouldn't do anything to be under suspicion again, and tying herself to Joachim would do just that. He had helped her escape Victor and had provided a safe place for her to stay until she gained her strength and was ready to move on with her life, but he wasn't the man with whom she wanted to spend the rest of her life, especially if he had problems with the law.

Tears burned her eyes. Tears for Joachim and his plight, but also for herself. She had made another mistake. She needed Miriam. What would her sister advise? After considering the matter, Sarah decided that Miriam would say to leave the area and to forget about Joachim, that he wasn't the man for her.

Sarah had to find a way to take Rosie and the baby home, alert the authorities and then find her aunt. If her aunt couldn't be found, Sarah would have to find a way to earn enough money for a bus ticket. She had to go somewhere. Home to Knoxville or south to Atlanta or maybe to Birmingham or Montgomery. She had to leave the area to get free of Victor and find a place where she could start over.

In that new spot, she would try to forget Joachim, although she doubted he would ever be erased from her memory or her heart.

* * *

Joachim peered through the bars of the jail cell. His life had gotten more complicated. Officer Nelson had hauled him into police headquarters, fingerprinted him and then ushered him quickly into a holding cell.

No telling how long Joachim would remain behind bars. His mind returned to Sarah with her crystal-blue eyes, silky skin and lips that begged to be touched. If only he could go home.

"What're you in for?" a guy asked from an adjoining cell.

"The officer mentioned manslaughter. Actually, it was a buggy accident that killed my brother five years ago."

The guy nodded. "Ask to talk to Sergeant Evans. He's the only sane cop in the bunch."

Joachim appreciated the tip. He would try to talk to Sergeant Evans, but as the minutes ticked by too slowly, all Joachim could think about was Sarah and whether she would still be at his house when and if he was released from jail.

Rebecca hurried into the kitchen and pulled biscuits from the oven. "Where is Rosie? I heard her talking to you?"

"She's upstairs with the baby."

"I'm worried about her."

"I am, too. That's why we need to hitch Belle to the buggy and drive Rosie and Joseph home."

"What are you saying?"

"This is our chance to get help for Ms. Hazel. We will take Rosie and her baby home and then find Levi in Willkommen. He said he would be working with his uncle at the Amish Market. Levi will know how to locate the police, a law-abiding officer we can trust. The good cops will save Ms. Hazel and arrest Victor and insist that Joachim be released."

"I'm not sure that is the best idea," Rebecca reasoned. "Rosie is weak and her face is flushed. I fear she has a fever. If so, she must stay here and rest."

"Then I'll go to Willkommen alone."

"You are a smart woman, Sarah, but you do not know about horses or how to guide the buggy." Rebecca wiped her hands on a towel. "Let me give Rosie something to eat, then I will get the buggy ready. We will go together."

Relief swept over Sarah. "We'll locate Levi. He'll help us."

"*Yah*, he goes often with his uncle to the market there. He will know about the police and who we can trust. I am frightfully worried about Joachim with the Petersville police, especially if Victor was the informant who called them. Think of how many lies he will tell them about Joachim."

Sarah took a tray with biscuits and ham upstairs to Rosie and quickly explained that she and Rebecca were leaving to get help and that Rosie needed to remain inside with the doors locked.

"Are you sure my baby will be safe here? I am not worried about myself, but I am worried for my child."

"You'll both be safe."

But would they be? *Please, God, let nothing happen to this young woman and her precious infant.*

Sarah hurried to the kitchen. She grabbed the cape off the peg and put the bonnet on her head and tied it under her chin. Looking around the kitchen one more time, Sarah saw the chair where Joachim had sat and the towel where he wiped his hands. Mentally revisiting the past few days, she saw his warm smile and the acceptance and understanding in his brown eyes. She had to say goodbye to his memory and to this home where she had found something she had never experienced in her life. She had found love and acceptance and the true meaning of Christian charity and a heartfelt concern for others. She would carry that memory with her forever.

Rebecca led Belle, now hitched to the buggy, out of the barn. With no time to spare, Sarah opened the door and hurried outside. Dark clouds covered the sky and blocked the warming rays of the sun, as if all of nature was mourning Joachim's arrest and the hateful crimes that had happened in the house next door.

Sarah needed to get help for Ms. Hazel and Rosie and the baby, and yes, Joachim, too. Then, unless she could find her aunt, she would leave the area never to return again.

She climbed into the back of the buggy, missing Joachim's strong arms to lift her onto the seat. She could no longer rely on him. She had to rely on her own wherewithal.

Rebecca had called her strong, although she felt weak and unsure of the future. What would it bring? All she saw was loneliness and sorrow in the days ahead as she began to realize she wanted to remain in this Amish community.

Did Joachim have something to do with that?

She nodded imperceptibly. He had everything to do with the way she felt and the sorrow that pulled at her heart.

# TWENTY-ONE

Rebecca was right. Sarah wouldn't have been able to navigate the roads. Belle was a well-trained mare, but she still needed a competent person handling the reins.

"Once we get on the main road to Willkommen, we will not have to worry," Rebecca said with assurance. "Belle will continue straight along that road, but first we must make a turn at the next intersection and watch for approaching vehicles. The *Englisch* demand the right-of-way, so we must be careful."

"I'll be on the lookout for cars while you handle Belle."

Rebecca reached back and grabbed her hand. "We must pray for our trip."

"Pray for Joachim, as well. I am worried about his safety."

"*Gott* will provide," Rebecca said with confidence. "And do not worry about Victor. He will not see you in the back seat nor will he recognize you even if he passes us on the road."

Sarah hoped Rebecca's statement held true.

Both of them bowed their heads and offered a quick prayer. Rebecca squeezed Sarah's hand and then flicked the reins. Belle trotted to the gate and slowed of her own volition while both Rebecca and Sarah checked for oncoming cars. Once they confirmed both directions were clear, Rebecca encouraged the mare onto the roadway. With another flick of Rebecca's wrist, Belle increased her gait to a rapid trot.

Sarah glanced back at the Burkholder farm. Rosie was inside with the doors locked. Hopefully, she and the baby would be safe.

*Lord, if You're listening, protect Rosie and that precious baby. Keep Victor far from them and let no other vile men come near the farm.*

"We must pass the driveway to the Thomin property," Rebecca said, as if reading Sarah's mind. "Just after that, we will turn right at the intersection. The road heads over the mountain toward Willkommen. Once we enter the town, we must follow the signs for the market. We will find Levi there. You can tell him what happened, and he will take you to the sheriff."

Sarah couldn't control her nervousness when the fence around the Thomin property appeared on their left. As if realizing her upset, Rebecca hurried Belle along. The mare's brisk trot made the buggy creak and groan as it swayed. Sarah's stomach roiled in sync with the back and forth motion. The Thomin driveway came into view.

Her heart stopped and a gasp escaped her lips.

She couldn't look away from the sight of Victor's red pickup idling at the end of the drive. He sat at the wheel, his gaze on the buggy as it approached.

Sarah lowered her head. The black bonnet had a wide bill, but would it hide her from Victor's view?

*Please, do not let him see me.*

Rebecca acted unfazed and unaffected by the red pickup. If only Victor wouldn't recognize either of them.

Sarah focused her attention on the clip-clop of Belle's hooves and attempted to drive out the fear of seeing Victor, knowing he could swerve onto the roadway, at any second, and brake to a stop in front of the buggy.

Thankfully, the pickup remained stationary. When the buggy was more than fifty yards along, Victor pulled his truck onto the road. Sarah recognized the hum of the souped-up engine. The intersection lay ahead.

"Get going, Belle." Rebecca flicked the reins. The mare increased her pace.

Sarah peered at the oncoming intersection, relieved that no cars approached from either direction. Instinctively, Belle slowed then stepped into the turn, following the slight pressure Rebecca had put on the reins.

The wind tugged at Sarah's bonnet. She raised her right hand to hold it in place. The sound of the truck's engine roared behind them.

Tires squealed and a blur of red passed on the left, then braked to a stop. Her heart hammered in her chest. Rebecca pulled up on the reins. The buggy eased to a stop.

The door of the pickup flew open. Victor jumped to the pavement.

Sarah's heart lodged in her throat. She looked to her left and right, hoping for some way to escape, but she couldn't escape Victor. He had found her once again.

Twilight descended over the farmland and painted the hillside in shadows as the police car drove along the country road. Joachim sat in the rear, fearing what had happened to Sarah and Rosie and the baby and his sister in his absence. How foolish of him to have considered, at one time, going to the police for help. They had turned a deaf ear to his recounting of all that had happened.

Thankfully, Sergeant Evans had come on duty at the end of the day shift. He had listened to Joachim and was sympathetic to what he had to say.

"I read your statement about your brother's death," Evans said, "and don't see any reason to hold you. The guy who brought you in tries to be a tough dude at times. He hauled you in for questioning, but there isn't any evidence to charge you. If we need to talk to you again, we know where to find you. I'll drive you home. Tomorrow I'll explain what happened to the captain who's been out of town. I have a strong feeling the officer who called you in will be disciplined."

Joachim was grateful for the officer's honesty. At least there was one trustworthy cop in Petersville.

When the police car turned onto the Burkholder property, Joachim should have felt relief and a sense of anticipation to be reunited with Sarah again. He would explain everything to her about his bother and what had happened that night as well as his father's anger, which had forced Joachim to leave.

Would she understand? He would not know until he told her how he really felt.

Hopefully, he would not be too late.

But when the police car pulled to a stop in front of the house, Joachim's stomach soured, seeing his father's face staring down at him from the upstairs window.

He had not expected such a homecoming.

Joachim stepped from the car. The officer turned the patrol cruiser around in the drive and headed back to Petersville.

*Mamm* opened the kitchen door. Tears streamed down her cheeks at the sight of him. Joachim longed to open his arms and run to embrace her. Then his *datt* eased around her and stepped onto the porch.

His father's eyes were hooded, but the scowl on his face cut into Joachim's heart.

There was no welcome to find in his father's expression.

"Is this the way you come home," his father asked, "in the back of a police car, like a criminal?"

His mother's faint gasp broke Joachim's heart.

"Once again, you are reacting without learning what really happened." The words of reconciliation Joachim had planned to utter refused to issue forth. Instead, he felt the need to vindicate himself.

Joachim fisted his hands, then opened them, consciously trying to overcome the frustration that welled up within him. "You were reacting to your grief when you closed me out of the family and forced me to leave home, but you were wrong, *Datt*. I had done nothing wrong. Rebecca will tell you. Have you talked to her?"

"Rebecca is not here," his father said.

"The only ones here are a young Amish woman who appears scared to death and her infant," his mother added.

Joachim tensed. "What about Sarah?"

Confusion washed over his father's face.

"Who are you talking about, Joachim?" his mother asked. "What happened while we were gone?"

Which was the question Joachim wanted answered, as well.

A sickness filled his gut and he turned in the direction of the Thomin home, fearing Victor had struck again.

Without waiting to explain to his parents, Joachim started running along the drive to the path that cut through the woods. His heart pounded in his ears. The rhythm of his feet hitting the ground kept time with the internal voice that kept screaming Sarah's name.

Victor had captured her. Joachim was to blame because he had left her alone. His gut clenched and pain cut through his heart.

Joachim had saved her once, but would he be able to save her again?

# TWENTY-TWO

"Where are you taking me?" Sarah demanded.

Victor yanked her out of the attic closet where he had kept her locked up throughout the past day. She struggled to free herself from his hold, but he slapped her face and shoved her down the stairs.

All around her candles flickered, their light casting eerie shadows over the yellowed wallpaper. The smell of smoke rose from below and burned Sarah's eyes.

Memories of her childhood circled through her mind.

She tried to pull out of Victor's grasp. "What did you do with Rebecca?"

Maniacal laughter was his only response.

"You're insane, Victor."

"That's what my friend George said. He thought he could overpower me, but I proved him wrong."

"George? Was he the man who had Miriam? You killed him, didn't you?"

"Like I killed Naomi. She planned to leave me. I told her to stay, that we would have a good life together. It's fortunate I didn't kill you, Sarah."

She fought against his hold. "I'm not going with you."

"Don't disobey me," Victor screamed, his hand tight on her arm.

"You can't control me," she insisted, struggling to maintain her courage. "I'm not the same person you held captive in your attic. I'm stronger now and I see things more clearly."

"You said you started a fire when you were young. You told me all about it when you were drugged. Your mother left you alone in the house with her boyfriend, and you hid in the closet with the candle. You tried to light it and the fire started. You would have died except Miriam saved you, but she can't save you this time, Sarah. You'll either die in the fire or go with me."

She squared her shoulders and raised her jaw. "I won't go anywhere with you."

He grabbed her by the throat and dragged her down the next flight of stairs. She tripped over her feet and fell. She tried to crawl away from him. He kicked her, then pulled her upright.

The air was thick with smoke. "What about your mother, Victor? She won't survive the fire."

He laughed. "Does that worry you? She doesn't die as easy as you might think. I've tried everything with her, but she's too strong. I stopped her heart medicine, then I gave her sleeping pills. I even tried rat poison, but I must have not given her enough."

"You can't leave her in a burning house."

"Maybe I'll come back for her later. After I take you someplace safe. A guy in Savannah wanted you, Sarah, but I bought you first. You're mine, and you'll do what I say."

"I don't belong to you." She kicked and pummeled him with her free hand. He caught her wrist and bent her arm up behind her. The pain made her breath catch. She gasped for air.

Her knees went weak and she fell. He kicked her down the steps and ran after her. She landed at the bottom of the stairs. Her gaze turned to the kitchen, where the man with the scar lay bleeding on the floor, his chest rising and lowering ever so slightly. That must be George. From the amount of blood he had lost, she was certain George couldn't live long.

"Where's the other man?" she asked, thinking of the slender guy with shoulder-length hair, the guy she had mistaken for her sister.

"Karl? He's in the basement, dead."

"Why, Victor?"

"Because I had to strike back at someone or something. The electric company said I didn't pay my bills, so they turned off the power." Victor fumed. "Don't they know I'm a Thomin? My family is the wealthiest in this county."

She had to get away from him—but he was stronger and could easily overpower her. Sarah's only chance was to distract him and catch him off guard.

She glanced up the stairs. "Look, Victor. They're coming out of the attic because of the fire. Do you see them?"

He glanced up. "What are you talking about?"

"The rats that live in the attic. They're coming down the stairs."

"No!" He slapped her across the face.

"They're coming after you."

"That's why my mother has to stay here. She never tried to save me."

"Save you from what?"

"From my father. He wanted a son who loved what he loved, woodworking and finance and this house. When I didn't fall in line, he'd lock me in the woodshed. You know what I'd hear?"

"You'd hear the rats."

He nodded, his crazed eyes wide. "At night, they'd crawl over me to get to the food he placed on the floor to attract them. I'd scream, but my mother ignored me. Now, everyone will ignore her."

Victor grabbed Sarah's arm and dragged her to the pickup parked near the front of the house.

She fought against his hold.

He struck her again.

Her knees gave way once more. He shoved her into the truck and climbed in the driver's side. He pulled a weapon from his waist and jammed it into her ribs.

"Do as I say or you'll die."

He gunned the engine and screeched away from the house. She saw movement near the barn.

Her heart lurched.

Sarah jammed her face against the glass and screamed, but he was oblivious to what had happened.

If only Joachim had seen her.

# TWENTY-THREE

Joachim saw the red pickup pull out of the driveway, going faster than seemed possible. While he didn't like the idea of the man driving recklessly on the road where others could get hurt, Joachim was still glad he was gone. With Victor out of the way, he could search the house and find Sarah.

"Joachim?" A voice sounded behind him.

He turned to see Levi. "Your father said Rebecca is gone and that you took the path leading to the Thomin home."

Levi pointed to the once-stately home. Joachim turned to see flames licking the roof. They started running.

The front door hung open. They dashed inside and climbed the stairs to the second floor.

"Ms. Hazel." Joachim pointed to her bedroom door. Both men ran to the master suite.

The frail lady lay in bed.

Joachim pulled her free of the coverings and placed her in Levi's arms. "Get her outside. She needs fresh air. I'm going to the attic where Victor kept Sarah."

He climbed the flight of stairs, taking them two at a time.

At the top of the landing, he saw the door and tried the knob. Locked. He pounded on the door. "Sarah?"

Why wouldn't she answer?

Joachim hurled his weight against the door, once, twice, three time before it splintered. He kicked it open and ran to where Sarah crouched, huddled in the corner.

When she looked up, he didn't see Sarah.

Instead, he saw Rebecca.

"Where are you taking me?" Sarah demanded.

Victor was driving like a crazed man. Surely they would wreck before they arrived at their destination.

"We'll go to Savannah and get onboard a ship and head to one of the islands. You belong to me, and you'll do as I say."

"I always obeyed you, Victor," she said, hoping to calm his outrage.

"Until you ran off. Joachim helped you, didn't he?"

Wanting to distract him from thinking about Joachim, she asked, "Why did you keep Rosie and not give her medical care when the baby was born?"

"She never told me she was pregnant. The people I bought her from didn't tell me either. I brought her home to care for my mother. Then after a few months, I realized the truth."

"Are you sure it wasn't your baby, Victor?"

"No!" He shook his head. "I never touched her, but I let her stay until she got too big. I was sickened that she would bring a child into the world."

"She gave the child life," Sarah tried to reason.

"The child didn't deserve to live. Neither of them did. Besides, I provided food and shelter."

"You call the root cellar shelter? You buried her alive."

"At least she didn't have the rats."

"How do you know? Did your father put you in the root cellar, too?"

Victor nodded. "My mother never questioned my father. Didn't she wonder why I wasn't sleeping in my bed? She had to have known."

"I won't let anyone hurt you again, Victor." Sarah made her voice sickeningly sweet. If she could make him believe she was on his side, maybe he'd let down his guard—giving her an opportunity to get away. "You can trust me."

He shook his head. "I can't trust anyone. The police captured some of the men I've worked with in the past. They're coming after me."

"What about Miriam?" Her heart swelled with hope.

"She's gone. I don't know where they took her. No one knows."

Sarah grabbed his arm. "Someone has to know how to find her."

Victor shoved her away.

Being sympathetic hadn't worked. Sarah needed to try another tactic. She had to get away from him somehow.

"Stop the car," she demanded. "I need to get out. You'll be okay on your own, but let me live."

"I can't, Sarah. You have to come with me."

"The police will find you. You'll go to jail. Let me go now, and you'll be able to get away."

"We need to stay together. I'll dress Amish. We'll live in the country in a small house. They won't find me if I'm with you."

Victor, with his hateful heart, would never fit in with the Amish. "You would stand a better chance on your own. You can save yourself," she encouraged.

"It's too late."

Sarah reached for the door handle. He struck her. Her vision blurred. She grabbed the handle again.

He wove his fingers through her hair and slammed her head against the dashboard.

Pain zigzagged down her spine. Her body went limp and darkness surrounded her.

# TWENTY-FOUR

Joachim hurried Rebecca through the smoke and down the stairs. “Victor took Sarah,” his sister explained. “I saw them drive away in his pickup. He acted like he was crazy, screaming about his father and rats.”

“Where did he take her?” Joachim demanded.

“When he was locking me in the attic, he talked about driving to the interstate.”

“To get there, Victor will travel along the main road. I will head him off by taking the shortcut. If I can get to the intersection first, I might be able to stop them.”

Rebecca grabbed his arm. “No, Joachim. Eli died there. I cannot lose you, as well.”

“Then pray I will arrive there before them, Rebecca. Pray Victor will stop his car and will have done no harm to Sarah.”

Levi met them at the front door and helped Rebecca flee the house and the fire.

“Oh, Levi,” she cried. “I never thought I would see you again.”

“I notified the sheriff in Willkommen about what has happened here, but I do not know if he will arrive in time.”

Joachim ran for his buggy, the buggy Sarah and Rebecca had taken earlier.

“Hurry, Belle. We have to save Sarah.”

The mare seemed to understand the emergency or maybe it was the flames licking the dried wood of the Thomin home that caused Belle to charge out of the drive and onto the roadway. Joachim led her to the bypass, the shortcut locals used that intersected with the main road.

Eli had planned to come home that night so long ago, but he had gotten too carried away with his need to prove himself. If only Joachim had stopped him.

The smell of smoke followed Joachim for some distance; the acrid stench hung on his clothes and filled his nostrils. Ms. Hazel and Rebecca were safe. Now he needed to get to Sarah in time.

He flicked the reins to spur Belle on and glanced into the night sky where stars hung like lanterns, their light helping to guide him.

"*Gott*, I made mistakes and cut you out of my life for too long while I traveled far from home. Forgive me. Forgive my iniquity and my prideful heart. I give You my life to do with as You will, *Gott*, but let no harm come to Sarah."

The wind whipped at his shirt. He tugged his hat down more tightly on his head and strained to see the road ahead.

The ride never seemed so long.

The intersection loomed in the distance. Joachim's gut tightened, the memory of that night five years ago played over in his mind's eye. Eli's buggy barreling headlong into the intersection. His brother's gleeful laughter as he looked back and taunted Joachim for straggling behind. He had not heard Joachim's cry of warning, nor had Eli seen the headlights approaching the intersection.

Eli had lived life on the edge, always wanting more than the *plain* life offered. He pushed at every chance to break the *Ordnung* and experience life as he chose to live it. Why had their father not seen the truth about his younger son?

Joachim had tried to save him that night, but Eli was too reckless and headstrong to listen.

Instead, his buggy had run headlong into the path of the oncoming vehicle.

Seeing it play out again in his thoughts, Joachim cringed, his stomach churned and he wanted to wrench the horrific memory from his mind.

Headlights appeared in the distance. This time, Eli was not in harm's way. Sarah was.

Joachim needed to stop Victor at any cost. He was willing to give up his own life so that Sarah would live.

He guided Belle into the intersection, then pulled her to a stop. He jumped from the buggy, hoping it would provide a barricade, and unhitched the mare, then slapped her on her rump.

"Yah, yah," he screamed, waving his hat and sending the confused horse running into a nearby clearing so she would be out of harm's way.

Joachim turned, seeing the pickup approach. He waved his arms to signal Victor to stop, knowing the crazed man would never do so.

If only Sarah would be safe.

# TWENTY-FIVE

Sarah groaned and blinked her eyes open. In the glare of the headlights, she saw Joachim. The strong man she had grown to love in such a short time. He flailed his arms, warning Victor of danger. Only Victor was the danger. He continued to push down on the accelerator and steered his truck straight for Joachim.

"No!" she gasped, anticipating the crash and knowing she had to act.

"Rats," she screamed. "At your feet."

Terror flashed from Victor's eyes. He glanced down as if believing a rat was in the car. In that instant with his guard down, she grabbed the steering wheel. The truck veered off the road, jumped a ditch and crashed into a stand of trees. Airbags exploded. Sarah was knocked back, unable to see. All she knew was that Joachim had been saved.

A warm trickle of moisture seeped down her forehead. She touched the wound and pulled her hand back, seeing the dark stain that covered her fingers. Even in her stupor she knew it was blood, her own blood streaming from a gash to her head that she only now began to feel. Gritting her teeth, she ignored the pain. She couldn't waste this opportunity to escape.

She tried to reach for the door handle. The airbag, twisted around her, prevented her escape.

The memory of being in the closet so long ago returned. She smelled smoke from the fire that had started in the main room of the tiny duplex. But thinking back on it now, Sarah realized she hadn't started the fire by her own negligence. He had. The man her mother was seeing. The man who was supposed to watch Sarah when her mother worked. The man who had gotten angry and forced Sarah into the closet. His anger had sent him into a rage so that he knocked over the candles he had lit and later blamed the fire on her, a child only six years old.

All this time, she had thought Miriam had saved her. Now Sarah saw it play out. Sarah had saved herself. Miriam and Hannah were in the adjoining duplex visiting with a friend. Sarah had alerted them to the fire. All the girls, as well as the neighbors, had been saved that night from Sarah's fast action.

Along with the clarity came a sense of relief. She no longer needed to depend on others because she didn't trust herself. She had made good decisions even as a child.

Smoke filled her lungs, along with the pungent smell of gasoline. She untangled her hands from the airbag and grabbed the door handle, but it wouldn't budge. She looked at the rear of the truck, seeing the flames, knowing she was trapped. This time she wouldn't be able to save herself.

"Sarah?"

Joachim was running toward the pickup. Flames curled from under the hood of the truck. He couldn't save her, and if he tried he would be burned and maybe even killed.

"No!" she screamed. Unwilling to have him sacrifice his life for hers.

Joachim knew he had only a few seconds before the fire would accelerate, sending a fireball of flames into the air.

*Please,* Gott*!*

Sarah stared at him through the passenger window, her eyes drooping as she became overcome by smoke.

Victor's head lay against the steering wheel, blood seeping from his mouth.

Joachim grabbed the door handle and pulled, but the door refused to budge.

His heart jammed in his throat, a roar filled his ears along with the sound of the fames licking at the truck bed. He needed to act. Now.

He grabbed the handle and tugged with all his might. The door sprang open, sending him flying backward. Regaining his balance, he raced forward and pulled Sarah from the truck. Lifting her into his arms, he ran as fast as he could away from the fire to a clearing, where he placed her on the ground, relieved to see her breathing in spite of her closed eyes and the blood that matted her hair.

He ran back to the truck, this time going to the driver's side. The door opened on the second try. He dragged Victor out of the truck and away from the fire, just as it accelerated, sending flames into the air. Burning embers fell on Joachim, searing his arms.

Leaving Victor well away from the truck, Joachim ran again to Sarah. Sirens sounded. An ambulance and a sheriff's car from Willkommen were heading toward them. Levi had alerted them. Thankfully, they had jurisdiction in this area near the interstate and had responded to his plea for help.

But would they arrive in time to save Sarah?

He touched her neck, searching for her carotid artery and fearing she was already dead.

# TWENTY-SIX

Joachim sat in the waiting room at the hospital, his head in his hands, unable to think about anything except Sarah and the surgeon who was working on her.

The doctor had been guarded in his assessment of her condition, using words like *dislocated shoulder, possible head trauma* and *broken femur*. Even more frightening was the threat of internal bleeding.

"We won't know the extent of her injuries until we open her up. What she needs now is prayer."

Except Joachim's mind was numb, and he could not put the words together into some type of a coherent order. The only word that he could utter was her name.

"Sarah" he kept saying over and over again.

Rebecca entered the waiting room along with Levi.

She touched Joachim's arm, offering support, then gasped, seeing the gauze bandages wrapped around portions of his arms. "You have been hurt in the fire?"

He shoved her hand aside. His own injuries were minor compared to what Sarah had experienced, and nothing, not even his sister's concern, could reach Joachim at this moment. All he could think about was Sarah.

"Have you heard anything from the doctor?" Levi asked, sitting in a chair next to Rebecca.

Joachim shook his head, unsure whether he could muster the energy to actually speak.

"I have been praying," Rebecca assured him. Usually, her prayer support would have touched Joachim, but at this moment, her words had no more effect than if she was talking about the weather instead of having asked *Gott* to save his Sarah.

His Sarah. He should have told her how he felt. Why had he kept pushing her aside, never explaining the way she made him feel, like a man who could face any hardship as long as they were together?

"Victor came through his surgery," Levi offered, as if thinking Joachim would get some closure with the information. "I heard two of the sheriff's deputies talking. They will guard him during his recuperation until he can stand trial for his wrongdoings. Not only is he a killer, but they mentioned a trafficking operation that stretched to Savannah and involved shipping women out of the country."

"How could this have taken place here in the North Georgia mountains?" Rebecca asked, sorrow evident in her voice.

Joachim heard footsteps and the swish of a woman's skirt as people entered the waiting room. He ignored the newcomers, intent on his own pain and concern for Sarah.

A hand touched his shoulder. He looked up into his father's face, lined with worry.

He blinked. Surely he was dreaming. Why would his *datt* be here at the hospital—and looking at him that way?

"I was wrong," his father said, his voice deep and sorrowful. He glanced at Levi and then Rebecca. "I have learned the truth about what happened that night."

Joachim did not understand. He rose from the chair, needing to stand eye to eye with his *datt*. Over the last five years, the father who had once seemed strong and self-assured had aged, his shoulders somewhat slumped as if from the heavy weight he carried. In his hand, he held his hat and with the other, he again patted Joachim's arm.

"Some things are too painful to discuss, son, yet I can no longer contain the sorrow I feel about what happened."

Joachim felt that same overpowering sorrow. "I ask your forgiveness for anything I did that night to encourage Eli. He wanted me to race him home, but this was not my desire. I was not racing. Instead, I was following to ensure he got home. But I should have done more—should have tried harder to stop him. He would not listen to my warnings, and I still do not understand why."

His father's eyes were filled with remorse as he spoke. "Only tonight, Levi told me that Eli had boasted about what he had purchased from some of the *Englisch* boys in Petersville. I do not know if he had taken the drugs, and I am grateful the police did not test his blood, but his actions were not what I would have wanted for him."

Joachim's heart went out to his father. Never before had he heard his *datt* say anything negative about his younger son. Eli had always been the favorite one who could do no wrong.

"You know he was driving Levi's buggy?" his father added.

*"Yah,"* Joachim nodded.

Levi stepped closer. "Eli did not ask to use my buggy. He took it without asking because I had left the singing and was talking with someone behind the building."

"He was talking to me," Rebecca admitted. She lowered her gaze. "I should have told you all of this five years ago, but I was too ashamed. You see, I was at fault for drawing Levi away that night so we could talk about the future. When Eli could not find Levi, he took the buggy without permission. I felt so burdened with guilt that I refused to see Levi for the past few years and I refused to reveal what really happened. It was only with *Mamm* and *Datt* leaving that I needed someone to help me with the farm. Levi volunteered."

"I am the one to blame," his father said. "Eli had not done his chores that day. I had found him in the hayloft with an *Englisch* girl. I told him he would stay at home that night instead of going to the youth singing. But when he asked again that night, I was weak and allowed him to go. I should have kept him home. I was afraid he would leave us for good if I was too hard on him."

"Yet, we lost him forever all the same," Joachim's mother said, stepping around her husband. She opened her arms and wrapped Joachim in her embrace. "I feared I had lost you as well, my son."

He smelled the sweetness of her and knew the fullness of her heart, which had always made room for him. Eli had been his father's favored son, but his mother had loved all her children equally, without censure. Joachim knew that she had never stopped loving him.

"My heart has cried for both of my sons. *Gott* has blessed me by bringing you home again."

"I'm sorry, *Mamm*, for everything."

"*Yah*, we are all sorry about Eli. He lived fast and died fast. As much as it hurt to have him taken from us at such a young age, it was *Gott*'s will."

"Levi has told us of all that has happened while we were away. How is the woman?" his father asked.

Rebecca's eyes were heavy with concern. "The nurse at the front desk said they will know something in the morning. She has been through so much."

His father looked at Joachim. For the first time in perhaps his whole life, he saw pride for his elder son in his father's eyes.

"You saved the woman and both Hazel and Victor Thomin, as well. This is what we were told."

"Victor has come through surgery. I am not sure about Sarah or whether she will survive."

He thought of the truck heading straight for the buggy, then it had turned sharply, leaped over the ditch and plowed into the trees.

"Her shoulder is dislocated and her leg is broken. There are internal injuries, as well."

The nurse came into the room. The sorrowful cast of her eyes made Joachim's heart nearly break.

"You have news?" he asked, hesitant to hear what the nurse would say.

"Ms. Miller is out of surgery and has been moved to intensive care. They're getting her settled. A nurse will notify you if she's able to have visitors."

Moving to ICU could mean her condition had taken a turn for the worse. Joachim swallow hard, trying to remain optimistic.

His mother reached for him. "This woman is *Englisch*?"

He nodded.

"You have known her long?"

He thought back to the first time he had seen her peering down at him from the window of the Thomin house. Had it been only a few days ago?

"I have not known her long, yet I have been waiting for her my whole life."

His mother drew him close and patted his shoulder. "I will pray for *Gott*'s will."

He wanted to contradict her and insist she pray for what he, Joachim, wanted. He wanted Sarah to live. Most of all, he wanted her to stay with him, but if she could not embrace the Amish faith, then she would leave the area and move on with her life. As difficult as that would be for

Joachim, at least he would know she was alive and doing what she wanted.

"When you were a little boy, you had little problems," his mother said, her eyes filled with warmth. "Now that you are a man, you have big problems that weigh upon the heart and soul. I have prayed for you every day of your life and especially over these last five years when you were away from me. I will continue to pray for you and for Sarah. Remember you must use your head as well as your heart, Joachim."

"*Yah*, that is true. But right now all I can think about is Sarah with both my head and my heart."

# TWENTY-SEVEN

Smoke burned Sarah's lungs. She struggled to breathe and tried to fight her way out of the truck. The door wouldn't open. She wanted to scream.

Then she saw Joachim. He was staring at her through the window. His mouth was open. Was he calling her name?

"Joachim," she wanted to shout, but she couldn't move her lips. Nor could she open her eyes or lift her hand. She was trapped in her body, in the truck, surrounded by fire.

"Sarah? Open your eyes." Joachim's voice. He must have opened the truck's door, or was she hallucinating because Victor had given her more drugs? She thought she saw the man from her childhood, her mother's old boyfriend, pointing at her and saying that all of this was her fault.

She thrashed her arm, needing to get away from Victor and the fire and the man who said she had started the fire, when he was the one who had turned over the candles.

"Sarah, it is Joachim. You are in the hospital. You need to lie still. Stay calm and rest."

She wanted to see Joachim, but nothing worked right and her eyes remained closed.

Her head ached. Her left arm felt weighted down.

A hand touched hers. She wiggled her fingers.

"That's right. You can hear me, I know you can, Sarah. I'm here with you at the hospital. I won't leave you."

"My…my sister?"

"What? I saw your lips move, but I couldn't hear what you said. Say it again, Sarah."

But she couldn't. She was too tired, and her mind was starting to drift. Hopefully, she wouldn't go back to the fire. She didn't want to be there.

*Please, Lord, I want to stay with Joachim. He always keeps me safe.*

She felt his fingers grip hers, then she slipped into darkness and couldn't feel anything.

The waiting room was empty when the nurse ushered Joachim out of Sarah's ICU room. "When can I see her again?" he asked.

"I'll come and get you in an hour. Right now, she needs to rest."

"Can she not rest while I am with her? I will not talk to her. Just being with her is all I ask."

The nurse's eyes filled with compassion. "I understand how you feel, Mr. Burkholder, but nonfamily visits are limited to only fifteen minutes each hour."

"But she has no family. She only has me."

The nurse nodded. "I'm sorry, but I still have to follow the rules."

Rules Joachim did not like and did not understand, even if the nurse felt they were necessary. He walked across the waiting room to the far windows. Staring into the parking lot, he wondered what would happen in the next twelve to twenty-four hours that the nurse said were so important. Sarah had been through so much, yet she was a fighter. If only she would continue to fight for her life.

"Mr. Burkholder?"

Joachim turned as a big man, probably midthirties, entered the room. He was dressed in the uniform of the Willkommen sheriff's department.

"I'm Acting Sheriff Dan Quigley. The nurse said I would find you here. Levi Plank spoke to one of the deputies when he was at the Amish Market in Willkommen. The deputy notified me. I'm sorry we didn't get to the Thomin house before the fire. Everything burned to the ground."

"But no one was harmed?"

"Correct. That's thanks to you and Levi Plank. Mrs. Thomin is being medically evaluated. She's weak and malnourished, but the doctors are cautiously optimistic."

"Victor was giving her sleeping pills."

"He was doing worse than that. The test results haven't come back yet, but the doctors believe that arsenic may have been involved."

The rat poisoning about which Sarah had been concerned.

"Nothing surprises me about Victor," Joachim admitted. "Is he still being held?"

"He's under guard here in the hospital. We won't let him get away. He killed two people today. We think there may be more victims. He'll stand trial in a month or two."

"And Ms. Hazel? Will she testify against him?"

"I can't tell you. It would probably depend upon the judge and how he feels about parent-child privilege. Right now, she's still too weak to communicate very effectively. With Victor out of commission, she would be wise to rent a room in the senior care complex located just outside Willkommen. That is if—"

The sheriff paused a long moment. "Tell me what happened once you arrived at the house."

Joachim recounted trying to find Sarah and instead finding his sister.

"Did you smell gasoline or any type of accelerant?" Quigley asked.

"I smelled only smoke, but the house is so old and made of wood. An accelerant would not be needed."

The acting sheriff made note of what Joachim shared in a small tablet he pulled from his pocket. He pressed for more information and pursed his lips at times as if envisioning what had happened in his mind's eye.

"Rebecca Burkholder is your sister?" he asked.

Joachim nodded. *"Yah."*

"She talked about seeing rats."

"That does not surprise me. Sarah said she heard them in the attic and the basement. I would expect that they ran from the house to escape the fire."

"You had worked on the house. Did you see anything that could have caused the fire?"

"Before my sister left the hospital this evening, she told me Victor had become crazed. Candles were burning. He knocked them over in his rage."

"Then he caused the fire."

"You would have to ask my sister."

"The electric company said Ms. Thomin had failed to pay her bills, and the power had been turned off."

"Perhaps that is why he lit the candles. Ms. Hazel was bedridden, but I thought Victor would take over payment of the bills."

"If there was money."

Joachim looked up. "The Thomins seemed to want for nothing."

"Yet Victor's father died some years ago. A house that size could be expensive to heat and cool. Money can run out."

Joachim knew that too well. He had had to watch his

finances over the last five years. “Victor planned to sell the home once his mother passed. He must have tried to hurry her along.”

Joachim explained about the scratching sound Sarah had heard and the root cellar. “You know about Rosie Glick and her baby?”

“I plan to talk to her next.”

“Talk also to Levi Plank about his sister, Naomi. She worked for Ms. Hazel until Victor came back to the area. She told her family she did not want to work there when Victor was home. Soon after that, she disappeared. The Petersville police thought she had left the Amish way and had run off, perhaps with an *Englisch* man, but the family feared foul play.”

“You think Victor had something to do with her disappearance?”

Joachim shrugged. “It is a possibility. A very sad one, but this could be.”

“I’ll check it out.”

“Will you also check out the Petersville police? Some of their actions have been questionable.”

Joachim recounted his experience with the officer who had hauled him in for questioning. “The officer’s name was Nelson. He mentioned Victor’s name a few times as if they were friends. I do not believe this man is above reproach.”

“The Petersville chief of police has had problems in the past. I’ll talk to him and see what he says about Nelson.”

“The Amish do not always trust the police.”

“Is that any police or just those in Petersville?” Quigley asked.

“In Petersville. Once trust is broken, it is hard to heal.”

Joachim thought of his own father and the trust that had broken between them. Eli had been loved, and in loving indulgence he had been trusted perhaps more than he merited, even after he had broken that trust. Regrettably, his father had given Eli another chance. If only Joachim could have prevented his brother from taking Levi's buggy when he and Rebecca were spending time together. Everyone had a little part to play in his brother's death, but Eli was to blame for his actions that night. He should not have died, but things happened and there was no going back to make them right once tragedy struck.

Joachim would carry the memory of that fateful night his whole life. At least now, he would be free of the guilt.

Once Acting Sheriff Quigley had asked all his questions, he shook hands with Joachim. "I'll be in touch."

"I have a question," Joachim said before the sheriff left. "What about Sarah's sisters?"

Tired eyes, a drawn face that hung low, a downturned mouth. Sarah blinked at the image.

A dream or…

He moved closer.

"Jo…Joachim?"

"Oh, Sarah, seeing your eyes open has made my heart leap in my chest with relief and joy. I have been so worried about you. Everyone has been worried."

She smiled weakly. "You…saved…me."

He shook his head. "You were the one who saved yourself. You grabbed the wheel and turned the car off the road."

"Victor…would have run…you over."

"I would have jumped to safety, but he needed to be stopped. If he had gotten through the intersection, I would not have been able to catch up to him. Or to you. The police were coming from Willkommen, but Victor would have gotten on the interstate first. He was involved in trafficking, Sarah. He could have known places to hole up. I would not have been able to find you."

He took her hand. "But you are safe now, and that is the only thing that matters. You must get strong and let your shoulder heal and your broken leg mend. You were bleeding internally, but that has stopped. The doctors were so worried, and so was I."

"What of Rosie and her baby?"

"They are both with Rosie's family. I am sure her parents were happy to have their daughter home."

Sarah nodded. "And…a new grandbaby."

"It will be hard for Rosie. She has been through so much. You saved her, Sarah. You heard her in the basement. If you had not insisted that we investigate…" He did not finish his statement.

Instead, he offered her water from the glass on the bedside table. She took a long sip and smiled with gratitude that he knew what she needed, even before she knew it herself.

"Victor's father locked him in the woodshed as a boy when he disobeyed," she said, her voice gathering strength. "He would hear rats. Sometimes they crawled over him. He thought his mother should have protected him, yet he loved her."

"Until she got old and he wanted her money."

Sarah nodded. "Ms. Hazel might not have known what her husband was doing."

"Or perhaps she was like Amish wives who follow their husband's commands within the family."

"You're thinking of your own mother," Sarah said, noting the sorrow in his eyes.

"*Yah*, but *Mamm* never stopped loving me."

"You father loves you, too, Joachim."

"I know that now. Mamie Carver was right. I had to

ensure pride did not rule my heart in order to reconcile with my *datt*."

"Does that mean you're staying in Petersville?"

He nodded. "For now. I want to make certain you get stronger so you can decide what you want for your future."

Sarah already knew what she wanted, but she wouldn't tell Joachim. Not now. She needed to rest and, as he had mentioned, regain her strength before she made plans. If only Joachim could be part of those plans. They still had so many obstacles that stood in their way.

She couldn't think of that now; now she wanted to think of the wonderful man who was smiling down at her. He had rescued her from Victor and from the fire and from the guilt she had carried for too long.

# TWENTY-EIGHT

Eight days later, Joachim stepped into Sarah's hospital room, hat in hand. "The taxi will arrive within the hour," he told her. "You are feeling up to the trip?"

She nodded, her eyes bright in spite of the brace on her arm and the cast on her leg. "I'm still amazed that the Amish are allowed to hire taxis. Are you sure the bishop would approve?"

Joachim laughed. "He uses them himself for long journeys. Our trip to my parents' home is not long in miles, but the doctors were concerned about your comfort in the buggy."

"Did you mention that I fell out of the buggy?"

"Some things need to be forgotten," he said with a twinkle in his eyes. "I did not want the doctors to question my ability to lead my mare."

"As I recall, it was my fault for not holding on."

"In truth it was my fault for not holding on to you. That is exactly why we are using Ralph's Taxi Service. Plus, his car has air-conditioning. The day is warm, but we will remain cool as we travel."

"What about your parents, Joachim? Are you sure they don't mind me staying at your house while I recuperate?"

"My mother has been cooking and baking for two days.

She always wanted more than one daughter and is happy to have another woman in the house."

"And your father?"

"He gave his nod of approval. Currently, he is busy in the fields. I have been helping him, but thankfully, he has not asked me to join him there today. He knew I needed to be with you at the hospital."

"I promise not to be demanding while my leg and shoulder heal. You need to help your father. I'll stay busy cutting quilt pieces and learning to sew a dress for myself. Rebecca said she would teach me." Sarah looked at the brace on her arm. "At least I'll cut and sew after my shoulder heals."

"You will continue to dress Amish?" he asked.

"Of course."

Her response warmed Joachim's heart.

"Which reminds me," she added. "The nurse said she would help me dress for the trip home. Can you tell her I'm ready?"

Joachim found the nurse and waited in the visitor's alcove until Sarah was dressed. She was sitting in a wheelchair with her leg propped up when the nurse pushed her into the hallway.

"Remember to follow the instructions the doctor gave you," the nurse advised. "He wants to see you in two weeks. Until then, have this handsome guy take care of you."

Sarah smiled. "He'll be getting dirty in the fields working with his father, but his mother and sister will provide plenty of help."

After waving goodbye to the nurse, Joachim pushed Sarah to the elevator and hit the button for the next floor up.

"Aren't we going to the street level?" Sarah asked.

"There is someone I thought you might enjoy seeing before we leave the hospital."

"You're being very secretive for an Amish man," she chided.

"Have you read from scripture that patience is a virtue?"

"Evidently, it's a virtue I need to master."

They rode the elevator to the next floor. Joachim stopped the wheelchair outside one of the rooms. He knocked. A woman's voice bid them enter.

He pushed Sarah into the room and smiled as he saw a very perky and alert woman sitting up in bed.

"Ms. Hazel," Sarah gushed, as Joachim guided the wheelchair next to the older woman's bed.

"I was hoping you would have time to stop by before you left the hospital," Ms. Hazel said with a warm smile. "Joachim has visited me each day and told me about your progress. I am so glad you are doing well."

"The last time I saw you," Sarah said, "I feared you wouldn't survive the night."

Hazel nodded. "The night of the fire." She glanced at Joachim. "I owe my life to Joachim and Levi. They saved me." She patted Sarah's hand. "And you saved me from my son."

"I'm sorry about Victor."

"Victor was a troubled child. My husband thought I was too lenient and insisted our son needed more discipline. I didn't approve of my husband's tactics. He could be an obstinate man and difficult at times, although most people saw only his positive attributes. Today, some might call him bipolar or manic depressive, which only added to Victor's confusion growing up. He never knew how to take his father. And I fear he inherited some of his father's infirmities—most especially the mood swings and the difficulty controlling his temper."

She looked down and sighed. "I didn't know about the rats in the woodshed. Victor never told me, and I'm sure his father thought our son should be man enough to withstand the punishment. Undoubtedly, those nights terrified Victor, and I pray he will forgive me someday for not stepping in." She glanced up with sorrowful eyes. "Hindsight is always easier."

"We all make mistakes," Joachim assured her, thinking of his own mistake. He should have remained in Petersville and dealt with his brother's death and his father's anger instead of running away. But if so, he would not have found Sarah.

She had taught him a lot about facing fear. She had returned to the Thomin home to save Rosie. Her determination meant the Amish woman and her son survived.

"I'm sorry about your house, Ms. Hazel."

"There's nothing to be sorry about, Joachim. The memories of what happened there were difficult. I'm relived it's gone."

"But where will you live?" Sarah asked.

"A new assisted-living home is being built not far from here. I've reserved an apartment and arranged for a woman whose mother worked for my mother to live across the hall. Her eyesight isn't good, but we'll help each other."

"Would that be Mamie Carver?" Sarah asked.

"Why yes. How do you know Mamie?"

"Joachim introduced us."

"You'll have to visit once we move into our apartments. Meals are provided in the main dining room. Come for Sunday supper once you're feeling stronger."

"I'd like that, but if you don't mind me asking, can Ms. Mamie afford such accommodations?"

Ms. Hazel smiled. "Mamie and I have an agreement. She'll help me with my day-to-day needs and I'll cover the cost of her lodging. My husband left me financially secure, which is a blessing. Because of his concern for Victor's poor skills in managing money, he made sure our son never knew the extent of our estate. Plus, I never gave him power of attorney, which is why he couldn't pay the electric bill when I was so infirm. That might have been a mistake on my part, but my husband had everything worked out with a lawyer before he died. I also regret letting the house fall into disrepair. As I struggled with age and my failing health, I left too many things undone."

She turned to Joachim. "There's one more thing I need to mention. Now that the house is gone, I no longer need the land."

The sweet lady smiled at Joachim. "You have always been a good neighbor. I'd like you to have the acreage, Joachim. You're just starting out, and property values are going up. Finding your own farm would be costly. I'll sell you the property for one hundred dollars."

Joachim's eyes widened. "As much as I appreciate your offer, that is far too little," he insisted. "I could not even buy a tenth of an acre for that price."

She shrugged. "My husband always said I wasn't good at math, but that's the price I'm asking if you're interested in buying. You'll have to build a new house, but I don't think that would be a problem."

"Thank you," Joachim said, his voice husky with emotion. "I will buy your land for that amount, but as I mentioned, you are too generous."

"I'm grateful, Joachim. You'll allow me to live the rest of my life knowing some good came out of the land. Perhaps you'll bring me fresh produce from time to time."

He laughed. "You will have your fill of tomatoes, beans

and cucumbers. In the fall, we'll gather apples from the trees. Sarah will bake you pies."

Hazel's eyes twinkled. "I like the sound of that. There's one more thing. Mamie Carver has a beagle who needs a home."

Joachim nodded. "He'll enjoy romping with our own dog, Angelo."

The older woman smiled. "Then it seems that we have a deal. I'll have my lawyer stop by your home next week to work out the details."

"I don't know what to say."

"You don't have to say anything, Joachim. Your actions have always spoken louder than words."

The taxi driver was a kindly man who was waiting for them when they arrived at the first floor. Joachim was quiet on the way home, no doubt thinking about Ms. Hazel's generosity. Perhaps he was making plans for his new home.

Sarah mused over his comment about her baking pies for Ms. Thomin. Not that she would question Joachim. There would be time later to talk about his plans. Now she needed to meet his parents. Hopefully, they wouldn't regret their offer for her to recuperate at their home.

Once she was healed, she would need to decide where she would go. She reached out and took Joachim's hand. Perhaps by then they would know what the future would hold.

The taxi turned into the Burkholder driveway and braked to a stop next to the back porch. Two buggies stood near the barn, and horses Sarah had never seen before were in the paddock.

"Your parents have guests," she said, suddenly worried about intruding. "I hate to be a bother."

He squeezed her hand. "A bother you would never be." After paying the driver, he hurried around the car to open her door.

"I will carry you to the porch."

Sarah saw the ramp Joachim had built.

"The wheelchair should have been delivered," he continued. "It will help you get around in the house."

"You've thought of everything, Joachim."

The kitchen door opened and a full-figured woman with big brown eyes and a warm smile stepped onto the porch. No doubt, she was Joachim's mother.

"Welcome." Mrs. Burkholder hurried down the steps and wrapped Sarah in a gentle hug. "We are so glad to finally meet you and to have you in our home."

A man, Joachim's height but with a thinner frame, pushed a wheelchair onto the porch. "Here is your transportation for the next six to eight weeks."

He looked like Joachim but with less bulk.

"Thank you, Mr. Burkholder," Sarah said. "You all are so generous and thoughtful."

Rebecca hurried outside. "Look at you, Sarah. You have color in your cheeks, which I have not seen before. Joachim, bring her into the house."

"I'm sorry to interrupt your company," Sarah said as Joachim settled her into the chair.

"You must come inside to meet them," his mother insisted.

Joachim pushed Sarah through the kitchen to the main room. She didn't understand his hurry. Meeting the guests was not as important as visiting with Rebecca, who looked like she was ready to burst with anticipation.

Glancing over her shoulder, Sarah saw Levi enter the kitchen, hat in hand. No doubt that was the reason for Rebecca's excitement.

"Here we are." Joachim brought the chair to a stop.

Sarah turned to greet the two couples who had risen from the chairs and were staring at her, their faces filled with expectation.

She blinked.

Her heart stopped. Tears flooded her eyes. Standing before her were Miriam and Hannah, her sisters, whom she'd feared she would never see again.

In one fell swoop, they swarmed around her with hugs and kisses and laugher along with tears of joy.

"How can this be?" Sarah asked once they stepped back to catch their breath.

"Miriam, I thought you were dead or taken by some crazed man named George." Sarah looked at her eldest sister. "And Hannah, I thought you were in Atlanta."

"I was until I drove to Willkommen to find you and Miriam."

"Only we couldn't find you," Miriam explained as she wiped the tears from her cheeks.

For the first time, Sarah noticed the clothing they wore. "You've dressed Amish?"

*"Yah,"* both sisters answered in unison.

"And we're married." Miriam tugged on the arm of a handsome man in black trousers, white shirt and suspenders. "Meet your brother-in-law Abram Zook."

"And..." Hannah drew an equally good-looking Amish man closer. "Your other brother-in-law, Lucas Grant."

"There's much you need to tell me," Sarah said as her heart nearly burst with joy.

Rebecca invited them into the kitchen for lunch, where they talked about all that had happened since they had last been together.

Sarah had never seen her sisters so happy. Joachim stayed at her side, eager to help when she needed something. She glanced around the table, realizing everyone she loved was in this kitchen. She had thought the past was over and that she would have to make a new life for herself, but God had reunited her with her sisters. At long last, the three girls were together again.

"We have room for you to stay with us," Miriam insisted as the afternoon waned.

"Lucas and I would love for you to stay with us, as well," Hannah added.

Sarah glanced at Mr. and Mrs. Burkholder and then at Rebecca and finally at Joachim. His face was tight with concern.

"This wonderful Burkholder family has been kind enough to open their home to me. I'll stay here."

"You've made a good decision," Joachim said as he squeezed her hand.

"I'm glad I can stand on my own two feet." Then she looked down. "Well, maybe not stand, but at least know what I want. I like being an independent woman."

"An independent *Englischer*?" he asked.

She shook her head. "I'm no longer *fancy*. I'm an independent Amish woman."

"*Yah*? Are you sure?"

"Cross my heart."

He smiled. "This is a good decision."

Joachim was right. Being Amish was a very good decision.

# TWENTY-NINE

Eight weeks later, Joachim lifted Sarah into his buggy. "You are lighter without your cast," he joked playfully.

"The doctor said I can do anything I want. My leg and shoulder have healed, and he doesn't need to see me again."

"This is good."

"Now tell me where you're taking me, Joachim Burkholder. You've been so secretive recently."

He laughed. "Just because I do not chatter on like Rebecca and Levi."

"They have much to talk about with their wedding this fall," Sarah said with a smile.

"*Yah*, they are both excited. This is as it should be."

"The wedding brings joy to the Plank family after the sorrow of the police finding Naomi's remains."

Joachim nodded. "Levi said Victor confessed to killing her because she would not stay with him, which is what he had told you."

"If you hadn't rescued me, Joachim—"

Before she could finish her statement, Angelo ran toward the buggy. Butch followed slowly behind the younger pup. The two adorable dogs brought a smile to Sarah's lips. "Angelo and Butch want to go with us."

"Maybe next time," he said with a twinkle in his eyes. "Today we will go alone."

He flicked the reins and Belle headed for the road.

The day was warm, and Sarah adjusted her bonnet, enjoying the sunshine and the blue of the sky. "Your mother asked me about my plans for the future."

"What did you tell her?"

"I said I needed to make up my mind about what to do and where to go."

"I thought you wanted to stay in Petersville."

"Hannah told me that help is needed at the Amish Inn where she and Lucas met. I am eager to see it for myself when we go there for lunch on Saturday."

"I thought we planned to simply visit with your family. I did not know you would be applying for a job."

"I'll see what the inn looks like and make my decisions then."

He steered Belle along the main road and withdrew into himself. Sarah didn't need conversation. She enjoyed the ride and being with Joachim.

"I want to get your opinion about something," he said, turning Belle into the old Thomin driveway.

"I must start thinking of this as the Burkholder place," Sarah said, taking his hand. "You've working hard planting the fields, but I don't want your woodwork to suffer."

"After harvest there will be time."

"The barn remains standing by the burned-out home site?" she asked.

"*Yah*, but I do not want to build the new house there. I have found a better spot."

He tugged the reins to the right and encouraged Belle up a small incline. At the crest of the hill, he and Sarah looked down onto a lake surrounded to the rear by hardwoods. In the distance, deer grazed and geese flew overhead.

Joachim pointed to a clearing. "I thought a house on the

rise would be *gut*. The beauty of the hills and lake would be visible from the porch."

She nodded. "It's so peaceful, Joachim."

"You like the spot I have chosen?"

"Yes, it's perfect."

"And you are meeting with the bishop next week?"

"He is coming for dinner. Your mother said I will be able to talk to him after we eat."

"You are asking for baptism."

She nodded. "Living Amish is what I want. Is that all right with you?"

"It is what you chose, Sarah. You are an independent woman who knows her mind."

She smiled, appreciating his comment. "And the Amish will accept an independent woman into their community?"

"My *datt* has already told the bishop that you are a woman of faith. My *mamm* has assured him of your sincerity of heart." He winked. "Plus, she wants a good wife for her son."

Sarah titled her head, her heart nearly bursting with excitement. "What?"

"She knows her son's heart." He wrapped his arm around hers. "My mother sees the way I look at you and knows how I feel."

Her cheeks warmed and she couldn't stop smiling. "How do you feel?" she asked coyly.

"I feel that life has no meaning without you." He pointed to the hillside and the lake. "All this means nothing to me if I cannot share it with you, Sarah. I love you."

She saw the truth in his gaze and felt overcome with gratitude. "I love you, Joachim."

He pulled her closer. "Will you marry me, Sarah? If you do, I will be a happy man."

"Of course, I'll marry you. I've been waiting for you to ask."

He smiled. "I thought perhaps an independent woman would ask first."

She nestled closer and lifted her lips to his. "First kiss me, then we can talk about how demanding I can be."

"There is something good about a woman raised *Englisch*."

"Oh?" Sarah raised her brow.

"*Yah*, she knows what she wants."

"Joachim, you're all I've ever wanted."

He lowered his lips to hers and they kissed. Sarah's heart nearly burst with happiness and anticipation of their future together.

A new home built on the rise with the water in the distance. Children to bring even more joy and laughter to their home, and a love that would grow stronger with the years.

The trip to the Amish Inn was pleasant. Sarah talked about wedding plans and what she needed to make for her new home with Joachim, curtains and quilts and the special dress she would sew to wear at their wedding.

Joachim smiled and nodded in agreement, letting her talk and thinking how his life had come full circle. He now had everything he had ever wanted with Sarah at his side.

They arrived at the inn to find both of Sarah's sisters and their husbands stepping from their buggies. Miriam and Hannah greeted them with hugs and then stared expectantly at Sarah.

"What?" she asked.

"I have a feeling there's something you need to tell us," Miriam said with merriment in her eyes.

"You know me too well," Sarah admitted. She grabbed

Joachim's hand and pulled him close. "We're getting married."

The women hugged and the men shook hands, and as they walked together into the inn, the conversation turned to wedding dates after the fall harvest and their new home and furnishings.

An older Amish woman greeted them in the dining room. Hannah introduced Sarah and Joachim to Fannie Stoltz, who owned the inn. "I am pleased to meet you," she told them with a warm smile. "The corner table is for your family."

Again the sisters continued to talk, planning the upcoming wedding and catching up on what had transpired since their last visit. The lunch was delicious, and after dessert as they sipped coffee, the talk turned to their mother.

"She is buried on property Hannah and Lucas own," Miriam told Sarah. "We will go there one day."

"I would like that. Mother wanted to find her sister, but none of us ever imagined that we would find a new life and a new faith for ourselves here in the mountains."

"I wish she could have connected with her sister," Hannah said. "I have a feeling some of her struggle and search for happiness was because of the family she had left behind. We've continued the search, but we haven't been able to find any clues."

"No one in the area has heard mention of Annie Miller?" Sarah asked.

Fannie placed the coffeepot on the table and turned to stare at the girls. "What was your mother's name?"

"Leah Miller," Sarah said.

"Miller or Meuller?" Fannie asked.

"Miller is all we ever knew."

"And what was her sister's name, the aunt you have been looking for?" Fannie pressed.

"Annie Miller."

Tears welled in Fannie eyes. "I cannot believe this, but it is true."

The girls waited expectantly.

"My maiden name was Meuller. Fannie Meuller. My baby sister could never pronounce Fannie, so she called me Annie. My sister's name was Leah."

"Mother must have changed her last name when she left Willkommen," Sarah said, putting the pieces together.

"Which means our mother was raised Amish," Miriam said with astonishment.

"And all of us," Hannah added, looking at each of her sisters, "have found our way back to our Amish roots."

Fannie nodded. "If what you said is true, then I am your mother's sister, your Aunt Fannie or Annie, whichever name you choose to use."

The girls circled the sweet woman and hugged her close. She joined them at the table and told them stories of their mother growing up, of her hopes for the future and her dreams of the family she would someday have. Their aunt also mentioned their mother's struggle with her authoritative father, who never showed his love.

"Mother searched for love and affirmation her whole life but never realized her three daughters loved her more than any man ever could," Miriam said.

Sarah smiled sadly. "And as her dementia started to take hold, she sought to return home to the sister she loved."

Fannie patted Sarah's hand. "I am sure she loved each of you girls deeply. Showing that love was the problem."

Joachim appreciated the importance and healing of the stories and the insights Fannie shared. The three sisters might have questioned their mother's love, but there was no way they could fail to see the compassion and concern that exuded from their aunt.

The family was growing, and Joachim felt sure that in the not-too-distant future, God would bless the couples with children so that the table would grow even fuller in the years ahead.

Going home that evening, Sarah rested her head on his shoulder. “What are you thinking?” he asked.

“I was thinking how God made good come from all the pain of the carjacking. We came to Willkommen to find our aunt, and we also found three wonderful men to love. I’m free of the memory of the fire. Miriam and Hannah both said they never talked about it because of our mother. She knew the man she was seeing had been at fault. Blaming it on me meant that he wouldn’t have to face criminal charges, so she forbid them to mention what had taken place.”

“Now you do not have to be afraid of fire.”

“I don’t have to be afraid of anything, Joachim, with you by my side.”

“Have I told you how much I love you?” He pulled the buggy to the edge of the road.

“You’ve told me, but I want to hear it again.”

“I love you more than myself, Sarah Meuller. You are my life, my breath, my heart, my soul. You are my everything.”

The sun started to set in the west as Joachim pulled her close and kissed her, which was what he had wanted to do every day since he had first seen her peering at him from the Thomin window.

“You rescued me, Joachim,” she said. “I’ll be forever grateful.”

“And I’ll be forever grateful for having you as my wife, Sarah. We have much to look forward to.”

*“Yah,”* she said, turning her lips to his. “*Gott* brought you into my life at the perfect moment.”

He nodded. "And *Gott* brought me home to find you, the woman I will love forever."

They kissed and kissed again. Then Joachim flicked the reins, and Belle continued the journey that would take them to the Burkholder farm. In a few months, they would marry and move into their own home where Joachim would cherish Sarah all the days of her life.

As if reading his mind, she snuggled even closer and sighed. "The pain of the past is over for both of us, Joachim, and tomorrow awaits us." Sarah thought for a moment and then added, "We have a lifetime ahead of us filled with blessings."

"Blessings and love," he added, and then he kissed her again.

* * * * *

Dear Reader,

I hope you enjoyed *Amish Rescue*, Book 3 in my AMISH PROTECTORS series (Book 1, *Amish Refuge* and Book 2, *Undercover Amish*). An *Englisch* woman and an Amish handyman are an unlikely match, but when Joachim Burkholder rescues Sarah Miller from captivity, their lives are entwined forever. Yet memories from the past continue to hold them back until their love for each other can no longer be denied.

What struggles hold you back? Turn to the Lord. He wants to set you free.

I pray for my readers each day and would love to hear from you. Email me at debby@debbygiusti.com or write me c/o Love Inspired, 195 Broadway, 24th Floor, New York, NY 10007. Visit me at www.DebbyGiusti.com and at www.Facebook.com/debby.giusti.9.

As always, I thank God for bringing us together through this story.

Wishing you abundant blessings,
*Debby*

## COMING NEXT MONTH FROM
## **Love Inspired® Suspense**

Available May 8, 2018

### BOUND BY DUTY
*Military K-9 Unit* • by Valerie Hansen

When Sgt. Linc Colson is assigned to monitor Zoe Sullivan and determine if she's secretly aiding her fugitive serial killer brother, his instincts tell him she's not in league with the criminal—she's in danger. It's up to him and his K-9 partner, Star, to keep the pretty single mom alive.

### PRIMARY SUSPECT
*Callahan Confidential* • by Laura Scott

Framed for the murder of his ex-girlfriend—and then attacked at the crime scene—fire investigator Mitch Callahan turns to ER nurse Dana Petrie for help. As they fight for their lives, can she be convinced of his innocence—and in his promise of love?

### RODEO STANDOFF
*McKade Law* • by Susan Sleeman

Deputy Tessa McKade knows the rodeo is a dangerous place, but she never expected she'd come close to losing her life there. Having detective Braden Hayes act as her bodyguard is as much of a surprise as the feelings she's developing for him. Will she survive long enough to see them through?

### PLAIN OUTSIDER
by Alison Stone

She thought leaving her Amish community was tough; now Deputy Becky Spoth is the target of a stalker. Her only ally is fellow deputy Harrison James. She'll rely on him to stay ahead of her pursuer, yet can she trust him not to break her heart?

### DYING TO REMEMBER
by Sara K. Parker

After a gunshot wound to the head, Ella Camden turns to the only man who'll believe she's being targeted, ex-love and security expert Roman DeHart. When her attacker strikes again, Roman intensifies his bodyguard duties. He let her go once; this time he'll do whatever it takes to make sure she stays alive—and his—forever.

### FUGITIVE PURSUIT
by Christa Sinclair

Schoolteacher Jamie Carter is a fugitive! But she's only hiding her niece to keep her safe from her murderous sheriff father. Bounty hunter Zack Owen goes from hunting Jamie down to protecting her and the little girl—no matter the personal price.

---

**LOOK FOR THESE AND OTHER LOVE INSPIRED BOOKS WHEREVER BOOKS ARE SOLD, INCLUDING MOST BOOKSTORES, SUPERMARKETS, DISCOUNT STORES AND DRUGSTORES.**

LISCNM0418

*With her serial killer brother out of prison and on the lam, can Staff Sergeant Zoe Sullivan prove she's not his accomplice before it's too late?*

*Read on for a sneak preview of BOUND BY DUTY by* Valerie Hansen, *the next book in the* ***MILITARY K-9 UNIT*** *miniseries, available May 2018 from Love Inspired Suspense!*

She was being watched. Constantly. Every fiber of her being knew it. Lately she felt as though she was the defenseless prey and packs of predators were circling her and her helpless little boy, which was why she'd left Freddy home with a sitter. Were things as bad as they seemed? It was more than possible, and Staff Sergeant Zoe Sullivan shivered despite the warm spring day.

Scanning the busy parking lot as she left the Canyon Air Force Base Exchange with her purchases, Zoe quickly spotted one of the Security Forces investigators. Her pulse jumped, and hostility took over her usually amiable spirit. The K-9 cop in a blue beret and camo ABU—Airman Battle Uniform—was obviously waiting for her. She bit her lip. Nobody cared how innocent she was. Being the half sister of Boyd Sullivan, the escaped Red Rose Killer, automatically made her a person of interest.

Zoe clenched her teeth. There was no way she could prove herself so why bother trying? She squared her slim shoulders under her off-duty blue T-shirt and stepped out, heading straight for the Security Forces man and his imposing K-9, a black-and-rust-colored rottweiler.

Clearly he saw her coming because he tensed, feet apart, body braced. In Zoe's case, five and a half feet was the most height she could muster. The dark-haired tech sergeant she was approaching looked to be almost a foot taller.

He gave a slight nod as she drew near and greeted her formally. "Sergeant Sullivan."

Linc Colson's firm jaw, broad shoulders and strength of presence were familiar. They had met during a questioning session conducted by Captain Justin Blackwood and Master Sergeant Westley James shortly after her half brother had escaped from prison.

Zoe stopped and gave the cop an overt once-over, checking his name tag. "Can I help you with something, Sergeant Colson?"

*Don't miss*
*BOUND BY DUTY by Valerie Hansen,*
*available May 2018 wherever*
*Love Inspired® Suspense books and ebooks are sold.*

www.LoveInspired.com



LISEXP0418